"This is what noir is, what it can be when it stops playing nice—blunt force drama stripped down to the bone, then made to dance across the page." ∼ STEPHEN GRAHAM JONES, AUTHOR OF *LEDFETHER* AND *DEMON THEORY*

"Benjamin Whitmer's *Pike* captures the grime and the rage of my not-so fair city with disturbing precision. The words don't just tell a story here, they scream, bleed, and burst into flames. *Pike*, like its eponymous main character, is a vicious punisher that doesn't mince words or take prisoners, and no one walks away unscathed. This one's going to haunt me for quite some time." ∼ NATHAN SINGER, AUTHOR OF *CHASING THE WOLF* AND *A PRAYER FOR DAWN*

"Without so much as a sideways glance towards gentility, *Pike* is one righteous mutherfucker of a read. I move that we put Whitmer's balls in a vise and keep slowly notching up the torque until he's willing to divulge the secret of how he managed to hit such a perfect stride his first time out of the blocks." ∼ WARD CHURCHILL, AUTHOR OF *PACIFISM AS PATHOLOGY*

"Whitmer's writing is swift, brutal, precise poetry, formed into the shape of people—breathing, hateful, murderous, vulnerable people that I care about deeply now. His characters are broken to begin with, and yet he breaks them open again and again, each time revealing a darker, thicker black sludge inside, and yet, this is also a story about innocence and trying to protect what tiny amount there is. There isn't a trace of sentimentality in here, but whatever tiny embers of warmth that are to be found in this devastated landscape (a landscape so bleak it approaches, at time, allegory, and yet remains disturbingly visceral), those embers are completely earned and the meager heat thrown off by them all the more valuable because of it. I feel covered in blood." ∼ CHARLES YU, AUTHOR OF *THIRD CLASS SUPERHERO* AND *HOW TO LIVE SAFELY IN A SCIENCE FICTIONAL UNIVERSE*

SWITCHBLADE

switch·blade (swĭch´blād´) n.
a different slice of hardboiled fiction where the dreamers and the schemers, the dispossessed and the damned, and the hobos and the rebels tango at the edge of society.

PIKE

BENJAMIN WHITMER

PMPRESS

Pike
By Benjamin Whitmer

Published by:
PM Press
PO Box 23912
Oakland, CA 94623
www.pmpress.org

Cover designed by Brian Bowes
Interior design by Courtney Utt/briandesign

ISBN: 978-1-60486-089-4
Library of Congress Control Number: 2009912456
10 9 8 7 6 5 4 3 2 1

Printed in the USA on recycled paper

For my wife, Brooky, and my children, Maddie and Jack.
All I can say is thank you.

PREFACE

The kid's left arm angles out of the dirty snow like a stick of broken black kindling. Derrick prods the body with the toe of his cowboy boot. Not a twitch. He holsters his Colt 1911, scanning the alley. The redbrick industrials loom over him, an ancient fire escape peeling away from the building, threatening to pull down the entire degenerating wall. Ahead down the alley, a dead end into a dog run, home to a pair of pit bulls trained to take chunks out of white cops. Derrick turns and walks back toward Cincinnati's Main Street. The morning still, his boots crunching through the slick snow in time to his heartbeat, cold and regular in his chest.

The kid had sure as shit known what was coming. Had to have, the way he played it cool right up until he caught Derrick with his face bent down over a flaring cigarette, then turned and broke out through the kitchen door, nothing but an Afro blur and shoe heels. By the time Derrick got his .45 clear of his holster, the kid was already ten yards gone, running for his life.

And he played it smart for the first four blocks. He stayed off the side streets, making a spectacle of himself to the locals. There were a few of them up too, sitting on their wrecked doorsteps, watching the scene play out through their beer-reddened eyes. A couple even stood, thinking to get involved. Derrick changed their minds, snapping his sights on the closest, barking out he'd shoot the first dumb sonofabitch to step in his path.

But then the kid made two mistakes. The first was cutting down the alley. That was the easy one to see. But the second was actually an error in judgment he'd made much earlier, probably sometime the day before, when he picked out his shoes. He'd picked elongated shoelaces that trailed after him like rattails. And he tripped over them. Fashion victim. Derrick stopped, steadied himself, pulled the trigger twice. His pistol jumped in his hand like something alive, and the big .45 rounds sent the kid tumbling forward like a face cord of dry wood in a hard wind.

He was twitching when Derrick walked up to him. His lips parted, his mouth and nose foaming blood. He was blinking, trying to speak, the sky pressing down from above like an invisible hand. Derrick let loose one more round, pounding a smoking hole in his head.

He's almost out of the alley now. Twenty feet to go, less and less. Two boys step around the corner, blacking out the sun in their winter coats. The smaller of the two whistles, his white face round and all but translucent in the winter morning, his thin blue eyes watering in the cold. An electric chill flashes up Derrick's spine, he raises the .45 on them. "Back up." They do, against the wall. Lazily. Unimpressed.

"Shot him, didn't you, motherfucker?" the bigger boy says, his big, brown fists clenching.

Derrick keeps walking, .45 trained on him. "Tripped over his shoelaces."

"That right? And just managed to drop his brains all over the place?"

"Could have happened to anybody. Could even happen to you."

"Bet we get ahold of you, motherfucker."

Derrick picks up the pace, no more than five feet. A wizened woman in a maroon housecoat and galoshes peers around the corner, checking the commotion. He shoves past her and he's out, jogging. Ironwork and stone storefronts. The sidewalk ruptured as if blasted by an earthquake, and the few trees lining the street blown over with sooty snow. The gutters and sewers awash with last night's beer cans and cigarette butts and one red high-heeled shoe. Derrick skids to a stop in the middle of the street, takes his bearings. There, the limestone façade and iron balcony of the Hanke building. He starts towards Central, quick. There are more of them now, a lot more, poking their way out of the apartment buildings, stumbling out into the street. He runs.

A whistle from back towards the alley. He knows better, looks anyway. The white kid with the round face. A beer bottle whips through the air, grazes his arm, skitters smashing on the cold blacktop. He runs. A howl goes up somewhere to his left. Another beer bottle slips in front of his face. Smashes. Then a rock. Derrick ducks, it cuts the air not more than an inch over his head.

He runs. His cowboy boots slide in the slush and the beer, he doesn't fall. His car's parked behind the kid's apartment. No chance of reaching it. He hears the cold snick of a pistol's slide being yanked back. He doesn't look this time. The gun cracks out four times in sharp succession, the rounds slapping the street off to his right. Gangbanger, never seen the inside of a shooting range, no chance of hitting him. Derrick barrels towards downtown.

Side street to his left, a blue four-door sedan sitting at the stop sign. Derrick bolts for it. A Mexican man in a blue pin-striped suit, drop-jawed at this lone man in cowboy boots being chased by a roaring, flashflood mob, spilling out of their apartment buildings now, pouring down the street. Derrick snatches the back door open, jams his gun in the side of the Mexican's neck. "Drive," he rasps, jerking the door shut.

"¿Qué?"

The mob boils towards them in a fuming mass. Derrick grabs the Mexican's chin, forces his head towards downtown. "Vámonos. Ahora."

The Mexican's foot finds the gas. The car squeals through the intersection, lurches down Main Street. "They looked angry," the Mexican says.

"It won't be the last time," Derrick answers.

BOOK I

And blended horrors stare before her eyes,
Even in that time, when all should be at rest,
When not one thought should discompose her breast

— *Blind Harry*

CHAPTER 1

~ You ain't nearly as big as I expected. ~

There's no trouble spotting Dana. She comes through the door leading with her greasy pelvis, wearing a pink winter coat that looks to have been run over by a garbage truck. A dirty black-haired girl skulks behind her, maybe twelve or thirteen, wearing a tattered sweatshirt an inch too thin for the weather. Dana's eyes land on Pike as if she knows him, and she shambles over and shoves the girl in his booth, then slides with her head ducked down like she's afraid somebody might see her. There's little doubt anybody hasn't. The diner's filled with miners heading in for the first shift, slurping coffee, rustling newspapers, calling to each other as they shoulder in and out of the cold, all of them with half an eye in her direction from the moment she stepped through the door. It's a small town, Nanticonte.

"You ain't nearly as big as I expected," she says.

Pike ignores that. "How'd she die?"

"Give Wendy some change," Dana says. "I saw a newspaper machine on the way in. She likes to read."

Pike digs a quarter out of his pocket. The girl snatches it, pushes past Dana. She's holding a gray and white kitten in her arms. It stretches its jaw and its pink tongue flicks out at the grease in the air as though trying to catch snowflakes, its eyeteeth like slivers of ice.

"How did she die?" Pike repeats.

Dana snuffles, wipes a long stream of snot down her pink coat sleeve. "She overdosed. Heroin."

It's not a surprise. But Pike misses when he ashes his cigarette at the ashtray. Tobacco embers swirl in the greasy air, rest sizzling in the thick black hair of his arm. He barely notices them. "When?"

15

"Last week." Dana reaches across the table and swipes one of his filterless Pall Malls and lights it with his lighter.

Wendy returns, a newspaper folded clumsily under her right arm. Pike ticks his head at Iris, the waitress. She elbows her way to their table, arriving at the same time as Wendy. "Take her to the bar and get her some blueberry pancakes," Pike says. He looks at Dana. "You need anything?"

"I could use some coffee," Dana answers.

"C'mon, honey," Iris says. She lays a hand on Wendy's shoulder, leads her away.

Every seat in the diner's full. Iris grabs a plate that's almost empty off the counter and tells the miner who had been eating that he might want to get out in the world and work for a living. The miner sits for a minute, smoking his cigarette and staring at her as if expecting she might return his plate. When she doesn't, he keeps staring at her like he might get angry about it. Finally, he plants his John Deere hat on his head and stands, shaking his head in amazement. Iris sits Wendy down, yelling out an order for blueberry pancakes. The girl hunches down on her stool, stroking her kitten's head, her narrow face pale and her wide blue eyes darting around the room, scared and over-stimulated.

Iris returns to the table with Dana's coffee. "She's adorable," she says. "Your daughter?"

Dana snorts. "I can't have kids. I was born with two uteruses growing against each other. I had to have both of them chopped out when I got pregnant after my father raped me."

Both of Iris's eyebrows raise. She turns and walks away.

Dana snorts. "Uppity bitch, ain't she?"

"Who's the girl's mother?" Pike asks.

Dana grins maliciously. "Sarah."

Pike nods. As if there was any way that wouldn't be the answer. "Did she find the body?"

"No, and you can thank fucking Christ she didn't. Not after what they'd done to it."

"They who?"

Dana shakes her head, shudders.

"I can't take her," Pike says. "I don't have anywhere to put her."

"If there was anybody else, I'd be talking to them."

"What about Sarah's mother?"

"Alice?"

Pike nods.

"Alice caught a case of lung cancer. She's been dead for years." Dana's eyes are like powderburns. "When was the last time you talked to Sarah?"

Pike draws on his cigarette.

Dana takes another drink of her coffee and sets her cup down solidly on the saucer. "No more of this horseshit," she says, standing. "I'm leaving."

"Hold on." Pike peels a twenty-dollar bill out of his wallet. She eyes the bill like she'd like to crumple it up and throw it in his face. "Take it," Pike says. "For your gas and your time."

She grabs the bill and fists it in her pocket.

Pike pulls another twenty out of his wallet, holds it between his fingers. "Where was she living?"

Dana wipes snot down her slimy pink sleeve. "In Over-the-Rhine," she says finally, snatching the bill. "Cincinnati, 400 Mulberry Street." She makes for the door, dragging the eyes of every diner in the restaurant in her wake.

CHAPTER 2

~ Iris looks at him like he's grown a second head. ~

Pike's face closes, he can't help it. He thinks of Sarah and blood pours into his ears like a vessel has burst somewhere back in his brain, flooding away the sounds of the diner in an oceanic roar. The patrons hush around him, a cloud of thick viscous quiet spreading out from him like an oil spill, but he can't stop himself from thinking about her. He stops trying. For a minute.

Then, "What's up, man?"

Pike chisels his daughter off his features. Rory stands over him, his square-jawed face screwed up in curiosity.

"You okay?" Rory asks. He's wearing jogging pants and a sweatshirt, a light sheen of perspiration across his blonde buzz-cut head.

Pike nods slowly. Rory slides in the booth. "Smile or something, before somebody calls a cop," he says out of the corner of his mouth. "We working today and I forgot?"

Pike shakes his head. "I had to meet someone."

"Who?" Rory's left eye narrows. "You ain't got no friends."

Pike fishes a Pall Mall out of his pack, his face slipping back into the funereal scowl. He rolls the cigarette in his fingers without lighting it.

"Not that hooker that just walked out of here?" Rory shakes his head. "Pike, you're old, you're ugly and you're mean, but even you can do better."

"What're you having, Rory?" Iris asks, suddenly standing by the booth.

"Heya, Iris." Rory gives her a boyish grin. "Half a grapefruit and a glass of orange juice."

Iris jots down his order. "I don't think that girl's ate anything in days," she says to Pike. "She's been through three orders of pancakes already."

"What girl?" Rory asks.

"That little girl over there." Iris points with her pen.

Rory cranes his neck. Wendy's at the bar, working over a fresh plate of blueberry pancakes, her snow boots hanging off the stool, dripping dirty water in a pool beneath her. "Who is she?" he asks.

"She came in with one of Pike's friends," Iris says. "The kind we always knew he had, but could never prove. Looks like she left her here."

"Rory gave you an order," Pike says to her. "Go get his food."

Iris taps her pen on the palm of her hand, looking at Pike.

"Fine." Pike sets his jaw. "Fetch her."

"Can do," Iris says, smiling big and turning on her heel.

"I think Iris likes you a little bit," Rory says, when she's out of earshot.

Pike ignores him, watching Iris talk to Wendy, ruffling her hair. Then she and Iris are standing at his table.

Pike clears his throat. "Do you know who I am?" he asks her.

The girl shakes her head, the right corner of her mouth twitching angrily.

"I'm your grandfather." Pike exhales cigarette smoke through his nose. "You'll be staying with me."

Iris's jaw drops over the girl's head, Rory whistles softly. Wendy just glowers. "I don't want to."

"I'm not sure how many options you have."

Wendy's eyes crack like twin windows smashed in a hailstorm, then flood through with tears. "Shh, baby," Iris says, holding her shoulders as she tries to wriggle away.

"Fuck you," Wendy says over her shoulder. She whips around at Pike and spits full his face. "Fuck you, too."

Pike peels his glasses off and wipes the spittle on his T-shirt. "You'll be safe with me."

"I don't want to be safe. You fucking pedophile." She drops her chin, her broad forehead looming over her raging eyes. You can tell it's the worst thing she can think to call somebody.

"Let her go," Pike says.

Iris looks at him like he's grown a second head. Then seeing he's not joking, she relaxes her hands and steps back from Wendy.

"Tonight you stay at my place," Pike says to her. "Tomorrow if you've got anywhere to go, I'll stand you the money for a bus ticket." He speaks slowly, enunciating his words carefully like he's talking to a spooked horse. "But you can stay as long as you want, too. The only thing I'm asking is that you sleep on it. Sleep on it for a night."

She stands very still, as though carved out of a block of slow dried ice.

"I'm gonna step outside and have a cigarette." Pike pulls on his work coat. "I'll wait for you until I'm done. There ain't much I can do if you decide to run off. But I'd prefer it if you didn't."

Iris looks at Pike like she'd prefer to run him through a wood chipper. Wendy stands with her hands folded around the kitten, tears and snot dripping off her pointed chin and landing in small sharp splats on her boots.

"Come on, Rory," Pike says, shouldering past Iris, his eyes blank and fixed straight on the door.

CHAPTER 3

~ It don't mean I like you. ~

Rory cups his hands to blow heat in them, his lungs contracting in the cold. "You don't think she's a little young to be put on the spot like that?" he says to Pike.

Pike hocks phlegm past a fresh Pall Mall he's about to stick in his mouth. "I wasn't any younger'n her when I started out on my own."

"I look at you and I see a man who could've used a little more love in his early years."

Pike lights the cigarette, the flame glinting off the gray in his beard. "When men thus weep their courage grows the less."

"Sure. That, and you're a weird motherfucker."

The door opens and Wendy glowers through it, her kitten burrowed down in her sweatshirt, its tiny street-crazed face peeking out over the zipper.

"I was hoping you'd come," Pike says.

"It don't mean I like you." Wendy looks up at him like he's a huge oak tree, stroking the kitten between the eyes. "I've heard my mother talk about you."

Pike smoothes down his beard, his scarred hand the size of her head. "Never doubted it for a minute."

They walk back towards Pike's apartment. It's one room in a brick industrial building that looms like a palisade over the small valley town. It once officed Anaconda and still carries their name in fading ten foot letters. The first flicker of Appalachian sunlight cracks over it like an egg. "So what's the kitten's name?" Rory asks.

"Monster."

"He don't look so monstrous to me." Rory reaches out to pat the kitten on the head. It hisses, its fangs flashing in the cold air. "Jesus," Rory yelps, yanking his hand back.

"Monster," Wendy repeats.

Rory shakes his hand as if to make sure it's still attached. "Does he get more friendly?"

"With some people." Wendy kisses the top of the kitten's head. "Not inbred rednecks."

Rory elbows Pike. "I think she insulted me." He's silent for a little while. Then he tries again. "So what grade are you in?"

"Seventh."

"Seventh," he repeats, as though impressed. "Seventh grade's a good grade."

"That about when you dropped out?"

Pike flicks his spent Pall Mall at an iced-over elm. "Stop setting yourself up, Rory," he says. "It hurts to watch."

Wendy snorts. Her face is thin and white, her limbs are starting to tremble with exhaustion. She appears to need all the venom she can muster just to stay upright. "You might as well tell the sun to stop rising."

"That's it," Rory says, veering off the sidewalk. "I'm heading home." He turns, walking backwards. "You coming to see me tomorrow?" he asks Pike.

"Depends on Wendy," Pike says.

"Bring her," Rory says. "She might enjoy it. There's always a chance I might get my head stove in."

Wendy doesn't answer. She looks like a flower in the middle of wilting.

CHAPTER 4

*~ Dingy and smoking and a lot smaller
than it looked last night. ~*

Three nights of rioting, there's no winding down. Derrick stands at the window of his fifth floor apartment, holding a glass of Jim Beam. Below the street's licked with the flames of a burning car, a pack of boys warming themselves before it, drinking beer and beating their good cheer on each other's arms and chests. Firelight and shadows flicker behind them, over the spires and ironwork of the Queen Anne storefronts, the arched windows winking at the rising sparks as if gleeful at seeing the city on fire. Given the cold, Derrick didn't think the riots would make it past the first night, but the mob just made its own sources of heat. He raises his glass to his mouth, drains the contents in one long swallow, washing away the taste of burning plastic with bourbon.

When he first joined the department he thought of the city as a river, as the big muddy Ohio that separated Cincinnati from Kentucky. Of each citizen as a tributary running into a common body of law, of order. He saw his talents as to channel it by force. He should have known better. There's always been different currents at work than he thought. Stored up in the ghettos until it bursts in an electric blossom like what's burning below. And whatever's to contain it, it ain't law and it ain't order. Derrick's learned that as a cop. The first time he found a six-year-old girl with her intestines hanging out her asshole, and her mother unwilling to finger her boyfriend. Him leaning on the wall grinning, the smell of shit still on his dick. Then picking up a kid for dealing pot the same day. The law's never enough and it's always too much.

Something moves in the hallway, scuffling, shouting, banging on doors. Derrick snaps out of his thoughts and picks his Colt off the leather couch, the metal and wood cold in his hand. He crosses the carpet silently, flicking off the lights. It scratches at his front door. Derrick yanks it open, drops his barrel. An olive-skinned girl wearing a pea coat, holding a baby. Derrick pulls her in by the back of the neck, locks the door after her.

"Behind me," she whispers, her eyes quivering.

Derrick nods at the couch. "Sit." He opens the closet beside the door, slings out a Remington 870 police model with a fourteen-inch barrel. He racks the slide halfway, loaded. He slides the .45 in his belt holster, then stands in front of the door, holding the shotgun in the crook of his arm.

And he waits.

The door to the stairs chunks open. Loud footsteps, three pair. Two of them built slight, the third bigger. They bang on doors, they shout out. Derrick cuts the woman a glance, she's on the couch huddled over her baby. He puts a finger to his lips. Then the hollow crack of a small-caliber gunshot, .25 probably, and the sharp peck of the bullet smacking cement. Derrick rests his finger along the shotgun's trigger-guard.

Then the door to the stairs opens and closes. And there's no more noise at all.

Derrick sets the shotgun down, turns to the girl. She's already on her feet, making for the exit. Derrick steps to the side to let her pass, but she steps with him. "Please," she says, her face blotched red with fear and recognition. "No trouble." She's figured out who he is. Seen his face in the papers, probably.

"No trouble," Derrick says. "Stay here. Wait for it to pass."

"Please," she says again, and she bolts past him, holding the baby like a football. Derrick doesn't try to stop her.

He stares at the open door. Then at the small puddle of urine where she'd been standing. Something cold and slick rises in the back of his throat. He takes his shotgun, walks back to the window, pours himself another drink. He leaves the door open all night, but nobody tries to come in. He wishes like hell somebody would.

Morning finally arrives. Cold, gray, quiet. The last of the rioters have moved off to better pickings, stumbled home to wait for the next nightfall. The car's laid out on the street like a carcass. Dingy and smoking and a lot smaller than it looked last night.

CHAPTER 5

~ *Set himself afire?* ~

Pike steps off the courthouse sidewalk to avoid two pinch-mouthed women coming out of city hall. And he almost grins, feeling the hatred roiling off their bodies. It's as natural to them as breathing, the way their kind hates him. They have ever since he was a dirty kid, greased to the elbows, tearing down engines in the front yard with his father. And it's sure as shit reciprocal, he's hated them right back ever since he was old enough to know what hate was. He even got one of their daughters pregnant, almost purely out of hatred. One who looked just like her mother and had all the same complaints. That really pissed them off. Must have. More than three decades since hasn't cooled them off. They've got long minds, these doddering old cunts.

He walks into Jack's office without knocking. Jack has a sheriff's head. A block of granite with the barest etching of a face chipped out of it. Just like Jack's father, posed in Jack's same uniform for a framed photograph that hangs over Jack's head. Pike sits down in one of the nail-studded leather chairs. "You got anything for me?"

Jack shuffles papers on his desk. "How's a few months of inside work hit you?" he says, his voice a practiced Kentucky drawl. He finds a slip of paper, flips it to Pike. "I bought it off the bank. I need you to wall it off for apartments."

"How big?"

"Big. Ten thousand square foot, give or take."

Pike folds the address into his pocket. "Got plans?"

"You figure it out. Make 'em all one bedroom. I'll get somebody in to figure out the wiring and plumbing." He goes back to shuffling papers. "How come your sidekick never comes in with you?" he asks after a minute.

"Gets nervous around cops. Somebody raised him right."

Jack chuckles. "What's his story?"

"He's a West Virginia boy. Hitchhiked out here when he turned eighteen."

"What made him decide on here?"

"He didn't. He was set on Cincinnati to make it as a boxer, but he ran out of money. I found him flat busted in the Oxbow, trying to beg a lunch. He's been working with me since, fighting the college boys by way of training."

"I hear he's good."

"It's hard to tell against these shitkickers," Pike says. "I sure as hell hope so. He ain't got a backup plan."

"What was he running from? When he left West Virginia?"

"Family trouble."

"Family trouble? Like he didn't get along with his daddy?"

"Like he was watching his kid sister and she caught herself afire on the wood stove. By the time he found a way to put her out she was burnt so bad she didn't survive the night."

"Blames himself?"

Pike nods. "A year later his mother set herself afire, too. Emptied a can of gasoline over her head and lit herself with a match. They got her put out, but she's in an asylum. Then there was his old man."

"Set himself afire?"

"Shot himself in the face with a ten-gauge."

Jack whistles. "I'd ask if he ain't got any grandparents, but I'm about scared to." He shuffles more paper. They both know there's more coming. "I hear you have company."

"Sarah's dead. The kid's got no one else to live with."

"You capable of taking care of a little girl?"

"I'm capable of anything I need to be capable of."

"I hope so." Jack looks squarely at him. "Don't fuck this one up."

Pike grins and his grin goes wrong. He pulls a Pall Mall out of his breast pocket, lights it and snaps his lighter shut, squashing the flame. "Did you know Alice was dead?"

"It was none of your business." There's something like satisfaction in Jack's voice. "You need anything for the girl?"

"As a matter of fact." Pike exhales a drizzle of smoke, looking at the photograph of Jack's father. "I need the official word on Sarah's death."

Jack looks at him. "You know something I don't?"

"I don't know anything at all," Pike says. "That's the problem."

"Why?"

"Knowing's the only thing I can do."

Jack strokes his mustache. Then he nods. "I'll see what I can come up with."

CHAPTER 6

*~ I woke up on the floor two days later, with a
headache like I'd been smacked with a tire jack. ~*

It's a big uppercut. It catches Rory on the tip of his chin and snaps his head back like he's been shot in the forehead. The kid who threw it claps his gloves together and bull-shrugs his shoulders. He's a big specimen, wearing a T-shirt with the symbol from an agricultural fraternity on the front. He's cockwalking for his brothers. He's got no doubt but that Rory's going down.

It ain't a bad uppercut, but it sure as hell ain't a showstopper. Rory's plugs the big shitkicker straight in the nose, crunching it like a bug run through with a sewing needle. Then he follows with an uppercut, jacking Symbol's head back, splaying blood in an arc over his body. Symbol collapses in a crouch, his face sagging like a sail short of wind. Rory lets him catch his breath. Outside the ring, one of his fraternity brothers whistles through his fingers. Rory hides his mouth behind his glove. "Don't get up," he says, in a low voice. "I do a lot of this."

Symbol shoves off his knee, stands. "Fuck you, redneck." He rotates his jaw back into place.

"Okay." Rory steps back a couple paces. "But fall anytime you want. Not one of them is in the ring with you."

Symbol rushes at Rory with all the grace of a fire truck. He throws a wild right lead, more of a grasp than a punch. Rory ducks it, shoots a hook into his rib cage. Symbol gives up on boxing altogether, brings his elbow down for Rory's head. Rory slips it and hooks the other side of his rib cage. "I'm gonna hit you with a flashy one," he whispers, clinching Symbol in the middle of the ring. "It's gonna sound good, but it won't hurt a bit. Drop when it hits."

Symbol grunts hate, blinking.

"Here it comes." Rory shoves Symbol back and throws a big

straight right with none of his body behind it. It catches Symbol cold on the jaw with a nightmarish pop. Symbol looks at Rory dumbly and blinks once. Then he collapses like a great big tower exploded from the inside. Three of his fraternity brothers jump in the ring and run to him.

Rory bites off his right glove, watching the big dipshit fake a return to consciousness. A mop-headed kid in a faded Kiss T-shirt lifts Rory's arm, does his best impression of a boxing announcer. Rory unwraps his hands while he talks, standing in the middle of the ring in knee-length gym shorts, feeling ridiculous. The ring's a cheap rental, set up on a stage that's used the rest of the week for country-rock cover bands. Nanticote doesn't have a college, but it's the only town in the county that ain't dry, so it has a college bar.

When the announcer's finished, Rory lifts the top rope and blinks out into the smoke. The open floor's crowded with folding tables and college kids. Four pool tables and a jukebox down one side of the hall, the bar and a few booths down the other. He skinnies through the crowd and catches the black T-shirt Pike tosses him and sits, sliding it over his torso. "How'd I do?" he yells over the college bustle and the Rolling Stones.

Pike's voice rumbles through the commotion like a bulldozer through corn. "You were kicking the holy shit out of him until he fainted."

Rory grimaces. "I was hoping nobody'd notice."

"Probably nobody else did. I've had my head kicked in enough times to know what it should look like."

Rory runs his hand down his face and shakes his head, shedding the adrenaline the way a dog sheds water. Wendy's sucking a Coke through a straw, reading from a large purple book. There's a full Coke sitting between her and Pike. Staring off at nothing, she slides it over to Rory.

"Thanks," Rory says. "That's just what I need."

Wendy shrugs without taking her eyes off the book. "I didn't buy it for you, I'm just passing it on."

Pike lights a cigarette. "Now, that ain't entirely true."

Wendy shoots him a look like she'll cut him into fist-sized chunks and feed him to a something rabid if he doesn't shut the fuck up. Pike closes his mouth around his cigarette and pulls smoke.

"Did you have a good time?" Rory asks her.

"I had cheese fries," she says, pointing at an empty fry basket. "They were pretty good."

"You're a tough nut," Rory says. He rubs the back of his right hand. It's starting to hurt, but not with the usual sharp twinge that comes after a good punch. It's duller, running down the bones in his hands like something cancerous. "What's the book?"

Wendy tilts it so he can see the spine. *The Collected Stories of Edgar Allen Poe.*

"You're as bad as your grandfather," Rory says.

She reburies her face. "How so?"

"You can't dig him out of a book, either. That's why he doesn't have any friends. Spends all his time reading weird books. Or insulting people that ain't read them."

Wendy's eyes slink over to Pike. "I doubt we read the same books," she says.

"I doubt it too," Rory says. "Nobody reads the same books Pike reads. I made the mistake of opening one once. Woke up on the floor two days later with a headache like I'd been smacked with a tire jack. Don't even remember what the hell it was about."

"That doesn't surprise me," Wendy says. "You being struck senseless by the sight of the printed word."

CHAPTER 7

~ Lost in one of the short, cold patches of sleep
that sneak up and sap him from behind. ~

On a Cincinnati side street, a downtown diner. Outside, a few salt-ravaged cars reeling though the slush, but no one on the sidewalks. The riots have been over for days, but people are sticking to the main roads. Derrick's hand shakes as he brings a cigarette to his lips. He inhales the smoke, chases it with burnt diner coffee. His eyes creaking in their sockets like they've been soaked in brine, his heart pounding its alien hammer-rhythm against his ribs. He can't take winter. He needs the heat created by people rubbing together on the streets. If he ain't hustling, he's got the stifled feeling he's dying. It's the mechanical cadence of his pacemaker. He's either on the go or he's passed out, lost in one of the short cold patches of sleep that sneak up and sap him from behind.

A taxi skids in the snow, turning sideways. The cabbie whips the wheel, straightens the car, drives on. In the booth across from Derrick a ground down redhead in a skirt eats dinner with a boy. He's a retard, a mini male version of herself that looks to have warped in the sun.

The waitress refills Derrick's coffee. She's a skinny black woman with ashy elbows. Derrick drinks, the coffee burns his mouth, he doesn't notice. He watches the retard. He has a walk-man on. Derrick can hear the song, Bruce Springsteen's "Working on the Highway," even over the dishes clanking and the griddle sizzling. The tune rolls around to the chorus and the retard's head weaves back and forth, his fingers tapping out the tune, his feet struggling not to pound into motion. His mother smokes a Winston, looking tired, looking like the varicose veins are the only thing keeping her upright.

Then the chorus hits, and the retard goes nuts. He belts out the words, his feet slap out the rhythm on the floor. Then he catches a gust of smoke in the face from his mother that means shut the fuck up. He trails off, his head shrinking into his shoulders. He doesn't seem sure what he's been caught for, but he knows he's been caught. But after a minute he forgets again. His fingers started dancing again, he's waiting on the chorus again.

Derrick watches the cycle through. Watches it again. The kid in anticipation, the kid bubbling over, the kid cowed and confused, the kid hurt. Derrick thinks about shooting them both in the top of the head. The song ends. When the retard thinks his mother isn't looking, he rewinds the tape. She looks like she's going to start crying from frustration. She pummels out her cigarette, lights a new one. The retard starts his cycle again like some kind of automaton.

Derrick's head pounds to the rhythm of his pacemaker. He quits looking at the kid, stares down at the green-flecked table top. Being suspended is worse than Derrick's superiors could have imagined. It's left his days brutal and thin. He can barely eat. His brain misfires like a rusty engine.

"You look like shit," Dick Fleischer says, gripping the table and pulling his gut into the booth.

Derrick blinks, brings him into focus. "I look like I always look."

"True. But you used to get paid to look like a shitbag, now you're doing it on your own time. Go home and take a fucking shower."

"You wanted me here. Say what you got to say before I shoot you in the neck."

Dick laughs out loud, his jowls jiggling. "Man, you ought to feel like you're coming up aces. The niggers have died down in the streets and as soon as we can get you cleared you'll be back out there running hookers and smack." He raises a hand to the waitress. "Pie and coffee," he calls to her. "Key lime."

"It was a clean kill."

"Sure it was. They're all clean kills." He puckers his fat face in thought. "Got busted sucking a neighbor boy's dick?"

"Raped his sister."

Dick takes a pie plate from the waitress, still chuckling. "I dig that you've got a moral streak, man, no matter how thin. But you're a walking cliché. You should try developing a conscience about something a little more challenging. Like wife beaters, maybe. Or pimps." He winks at Derrick and crams a forkful of green pie into his mouth, swallows it without chewing. "You know what one of the theories going around is? That the nigger was one of your dealers." His eyes scrape all over Derrick's face. "That he shorted you money."

"Say what you've got to say," Derrick repeats. "Then take a walk. You might think I'm joking about shooting you, but it's a point you don't want to press."

Dick snorts, blowing green chunks of pie on his shit-colored tie. "Don't threaten me, boy. Me and the union's the only thing keeping you in a job."

"What's keeping me in a job is I make arrests."

Dick wipes his mouth on his paper napkin. "And someday we're gonna have a discussion as to your methods."

Derrick rubs his eyes with his thumb and forefinger. "For the last time, what was it you wanted to tell me?"

Dick grips the edge of the table and pulls himself out of the booth. "Get out of town," he says. "We're trying to salvage what little reputation you got left. The real you ain't oughtta be here to collide with the you we're trying to create."

Derrick watches him squeeze through the door. Then turns his eyes back on the window. A brick parking structure across the street, behind it the backside of the new Proctor & Gamble building, its twin stubs like missile silos. Or a pair of fake tits. The rendering of pig's fat into soap. Exhaustion. Then a sudden rush of darkness from behind the building, starting from a pinpoint spot over the left stub and expanding to fill the sky. It's a cloud. Like darkness itself, like the sky lowering. Like South Dakota, when he couldn't stop driving. Cooking baloney sandwiches in a skillet over a fire by the side of the road, sleeping in the car. Spending the days staring into the prairie tallgrass, watching the mule deer and the pronghorn graze. Listening to the coyotes call at night. The morning sun rising like a flood up the spires, rushing through the ravines like bloody water. The clay and mudstone pulsating, the sun pumping aloft. Hell with the flames put out, a landscape that washed away every time it rained. Everything changing with every storm, nothing changed ever. Driving the same highway loops until every pinnacle and every ravine was burned into his brain.

"You can't sleep here," the waitress says.

Derrick turns to her and tries to open his eyes. But they're open. "I was just leaving."

Her eyes glitter blackly in her head. "Don't let me stop you."

CHAPTER 8

~ The bulb of some purple black fruit in his palm. ~

A cabin on the outskirts of town, in a small wooded clearing just off a winding logging trail. It was once a hunting shack, years ago, before the deer were all hunted out. Across the trail and past a rusty barbwire fence, a snow-blanketed meadow opens out of the woods. The sun's falling over the horizon and it's almost dark, the early winter evening coming on. The smudges of light escaping the cabin's windows flit like summer insects over the snowbanks and the tarp covered woodpile.

The floor of the cabin is open. A pot-bellied stove, a writing desk and an iron bed the only furniture. A kerosene lantern sputtering on the windowsill. Rory's just finished with the dumbbells, and is looking his hand over, the back of it bruised a rich purple like it's been pounded with a ball peen hammer. He clenches it gently and lets a warm wave of pain wash up his arm. Please don't be broken. At least a hundred dollars to get an x-ray, probably twice that to get it fixed.

He clenches his fist again, hard this time. The bruise darkens, he feels his forehead burst with sweat. He rotates the hand, he doesn't feel anything shifting that shouldn't shift. So, he relaxes, swallowing away a wave of nausea. Probably just fractured. I'll take it easy next fight. Let my left do most of the work. He pulls on a gray hooded sweatshirt and a pair of Redwing Loggers, and he's out the door, loping easily down the trail. It's dark and wild, overgrown, but he knows it by heart. The stars above flicker like knife holes of light punched through a black curtain.

Then he's out of the woods, cutting left on the highway, trudging the ditch towards the Green Frog Café, squatting on Highway 29 like a malignant toad a quarter mile before you enter the yellow spill of the town's lights. It's a cement bunker of a building, flat roofed with a gravel parking lot, and a front door that lets into a dimly lit foyer. Rory waves into the one-way mirror, the steel door buzzes open, and the bartender raises his right hand by way of greeting. He's leaning on the bar, his left arm in a sling, his ravaged face under-lit by the sink's light. "Howdy Leroy," Rory says, nodding at the sling. "What in the hell'd you do?"

Leroy grins woefully. "Everything I could."

Rory chuckles and keeps walking, past a table of longhaired rednecks playing seven card stud. "Boys," he says by way of greeting. The man he's looking for leans over the pool table at the back of the bar. He's tall and thick-built with gearhead muscle, his light blonde hair flowing down his leather Harley vest and ending at his belt. A hard case biker type sits next to him, tilted back in his chair with his boots up on the edge of the table, his stringy hair slicking down his face like black water running down the slope of a mountain.

Cotton turns to meet him, stroking his Fu Manchu mustache. "Hello Rory," he says in a genial roadhouse drawl. His handshake is long and compelling. "What can I do for you?"

"Just jogging by." Rory shrugs as though his being in the bar was an afterthought. "Thought I'd stop in and pick up something for my hand."

Cotton nods agreeably. "Sure. What do you need?"

Hard Case kicks his feet off the table and walks past them to the bar, clapping Cotton on the back. His face looks like its been banged out of rough flint with a sledgehammer. "Need a drink?" His voice is the same Kentucky drawl as Cotton's, but thinner, harder, with all the warmth gone.

"Maker's Mark," Cotton says. "And two Cokes."

Rory waits for Hard Case to make it out of earshot. "Say, thirty Vikes. Forties."

"Can do." Cotton hooks his road-scarred leather jacket off a stool and picks a plastic bag out of the inside pocket. He tosses it on the pool table. "Get what you need."

Rory counts the pills out carefully, making a show of it for Cotton. It takes him too long. The yellow light in the joint slows everything down. It's murky, specked with dark spots, the bodies of insects stuck in the hanging lamps. It's like living in a beerglass. Rory loses count. Starts again. Finally finishes, and hands his money to Cotton.

Cotton passes Rory a Coke from Hard Case, just returned from the bar. "What happened to your hand?" he asks.

Rory holds it up to show the bruise. "Threw a stupid punch."

"Rory's our neighborhood fight night champion," Cotton says to Hard Case. "One of these days he's going on to be the next Rocky Marciano, but right now he keeps the college boys in line."

"Heard all about it," Hard Case says. "You ever fight anybody that fights back?"

Rory chases two pills with Coke. "I fight anybody that shows up."

"I might show up some day."

"I ain't lost yet."

"Settle down," Cotton says to Hard Case. "This kid's one of the good guys." He winks at Rory. "Scary motherfucker ain't he?"

"Sure." Rory chucks his chin at Leroy. "What's that all about?"

"Arnold Kaplin. Stuck him in the arm with a screwdriver."

"Right here? In the bar?"

Cotton nods.

"Why?"

"No reason at all. He was drinking at the bar and Leroy came by to empty his ashtray. Just jumped up and stabbed him."

"Damn. What'd Leroy do?"

"Bled," Hard Case says.

Cotton ignores that. "He didn't have time to do anything," he says. He flicks his eyes at Hard Case. "This motherfucker had already taken the screwdriver and stuck Arnold through his left eye."

Rory winces. "Arnold all right?"

"He's a little pissed off, I'll bet," Hard Case says.

Rory nods. "That's too bad," he says to Cotton, "he ain't a bad sort."

"If he's got any sense, he'll be appreciating that I left him his right eye," Hard Case says. "And that I didn't stir around in his brains a little."

Rory nods again, without looking at him.

"You get everything you need?" Cotton says.

"Yessir. I think so."

"Vicodin's more powerful than it gets credit for. You be careful. I'm not gonna be the one to put the brakes on your boxing career."

"I take them for the pain now and then. And maybe a couple on the weekends. I don't drink or nothing, it's the only thing I do."

Cotton sets his bourbon glass down, empty, his eyes locking on Rory's as though estimating the truthfulness of that statement. "Then have a good weekend," he says.

CHAPTER 9

~ Nothing worse than it already is. ~

The afternoon sun shines in streaks through the parlor's yellow windows, blossoming on the drywall dust that drifts like ragweed through the air. Rory lifts off his dust-mask and sags against one of the walls, slapping the dust off his arms and chest, then plugging his left nostril with his thumb and blowing a clot of snot and drywall paste on the floor.

Pike's already sitting, his back against one of the water-damaged walls they haven't got to yet. He lobs a bottle of Coke to Rory and follows it with a sandwich wrapped in cellophane.

Rory looks the sandwich over.

"Roast beef." Pike holds his up. "Wendy made the mustard."

Rory thumbs for the edge of the cling wrap. "She made the mustard?"

Pike sets his sandwich on his lunch pail and lights a cigarette. "She said condiments were the only thing she was gonna learn how to make." He snaps his lighter shut on his knee, sending up a puff of drywall dust. "Got a real kick out of it too."

"The kid's weird." Rory sniffs the sandwich, takes a bite. "Pretty good mustard though," he says through a full mouth.

Pike smokes his cigarette, his eyes like still gray water.

"What?" Rory says.

Pike shakes his head. "I can't figure out a couple of things. About Wendy's mother."

"Like?" Rory sucks mustard off his filthy thumb, takes another bite.

"Yeah. Like?" Jack says, standing in the doorway all of a sudden. The sandwich turns into a lump of clay in Rory's mouth.

"What do you need, Jack?" Pike asks.

Jack leans in the doorway, his .38 slung low on his hip, cowboy style. "Stopped by to see how the work was going."

"It's going. Most of the drywall's in pisspoor shape, but the cross-beams are fine."

Jack looks around, nodding. "Good to hear."

Pike leaks smoke out of his tight mouth. "What do you need?"

"I got the answer to that question you asked me." Jack nods at Rory. "Think he can handle himself alone for a couple minutes?"

"You can talk in front of him," Pike says.

"Your call." Jack crosses his arms. "It was a heroin overdose, no doubt about it. They found her in the kitchen of her house, the needle still in her hand."

"Who found her?"

"A homicide cop by the name of Christopher Vollmann. He got word about a dead woman. A local junky told him, I couldn't get his name." Jack opens his mouth to continue, then shuts it.

"Go ahead," Pike says.

"They found semen." Jack spits on the floor. "They're pretty sure all of it came post mortem."

Pike thumbs his glasses up his nose, his face unchanged. "That's how word got out? The bums were taking turns on her body?"

"That's my best guess. Nothing worse than it already is." Jack clears his throat, and pauses for a minute. "Now, I got a question for you," he says.

"Go ahead."

Jack's voice roughens slightly. "Iris left me."

"I know it."

"The whole goddamn town knows it. Any idea where she's living?"

"How would I know?"

Jack looks him in the face. "I know you two talk."

Pike stubs his cigarette out on his boot heel and picks up his sand-wich. "I say hello to her over breakfast, like you."

"Well. Next time you talk to her, tell her to come on back whenever she likes."

"Whatever you say."

Jack turns and leaves, sagging a little like his backbone's missing a vertebra or two at the base of his spine.

Rory waits for the outside door to slam shut. "You know where she's at, don't you?"

Pike chews his sandwich thoughtfully, trying to get the hang of the taste. "She came up with a dead aunt. Took over her place. I hung a reinforced door on it for her last week. It ain't a goddamn bit of his business, though."

"You and him got something weird going on."

"He knew my wife."

"Yeah? Well he's got me beat. I didn't even know you had a wife."

"Well." Pike watches the dust drift in the sunfilled air. "That was a long time ago."

"You know it's like a local legend where you went to when you run off. I've heard all kind of guesses."

"I've heard them too."

"How long was it you was gone? Ten years? Fifteen?"

Pike finishes his sandwich and balls up the plastic wrap. "Keep pumping me, you might get to disappear yourself."

Rory laughs.

CHAPTER 10

~ His eyes like gasoline on oil and his thin lips drawn tight. ~

Derrick's driving, and when Derrick's driving, he's plotting. His hand taking part with the wheel and his blood revving like it's driven by an engine, the alternator in his chest joining with the cold mechanical cadence of the Monte Carlo's pistons. It was the driving that kept him being a cop long after he knew better. Wheeling his car around Cincinnati, owning the town. Knowing every back alley and side street, every shadow he's heaped a body in. You can't own a city by living in it, just like you can't own a mountain by building a house on it. No matter what the coal-rich assholes around here think, with their McMansions plugged back in our hollows, sucking the coal out of the Appalachians. Anything you own around here, you own by putting blood in it.

Then he's on Nanticote's Main Street. And he sees Rory through the front window of the Oxbow, sitting in a booth across from a grizzled old man wearing glasses, a girl perched like a cat next to him, reading from a book as big as her torso. Derrick careens the Monte Carlo to the curb and kicks out the door, the big December moon standing above him like a great frigid eye.

Rory turns his head to look at him as he opens the door. Derrick walks to the counter, stands as though waiting for service. The haggard blonde waitress is cooking. She flips a pat of butter skittering, burning across the grill, cracks an egg over it, lets it settle and scorch. Breakfast all day. The air over the grill thickens and warps like a living amoeba.

"You fight tonight?" Derrick asks, standing with his hands on the counter, not looking at the kid.

"Yep," the kid answers.

"He any good?"

"Golden gloves."

"Did you win?"

"I ain't never lost."

Derrick turns to face him, hitching his thumbs in his belt. He knows he's gonna take the little fucker apart someday. It's a thought that cracks his face in a rictus-like grin. "How's the hand?"

Rory shows it to him, wrapped tight in an Ace bandage. "Never had to use it once."

"That a fact?" Derrick notices the old man staring at him, his eyes like gasoline on oil, his thin lips drawn tight. He's bigger up close. "You got something to say?"

Pike smokes his cigarette. "I know you?"

"Derrick Krieger. I grew up in this little shithole. I heard about you all my life."

Pike's eyes skim off of him like a fly off a shit puddle. He ashes his cigarette, blue smoke streaming out of his nose. "You want something with Rory, Derrick?"

Derrick reaches under his leather jacket, quick, and tosses a bag of pills on Rory's chest. "A congratulations gift," he says, grinning around the table. Then his eyes land on the girl. And for the first time, he sees her face clearly. "Well," he says softly. "What's your name?"

A kitten pokes its head out from the girl's sweatshirt, as if checking to see what all the commotion's about. The girl strokes its head gently. "None of your fucking business, pedophile," she says sweetly.

"You look familiar," Derrick says.

Rory tosses the pills back at Derrick. The bag hits him in the arm, falls on the floor. "Time for you to go," Rory says, starting to stand.

Derrick nods, still staring at the girl. There's something he can't put his finger on, something dredging through the murk of his memory, gliding towards the surface. "Maybe it is," he says. He turns and walks to the door.

CHAPTER 11

~ These memories contain their own engines. ~

Pike's '64 Ford pickup chugs smoke, rumbling over the rutted logging road away from Rory's shack, the fiberglass cap rocking and pinging on the bed. He gears up onto Highway 29, slugging out through the slush and gray salt towards Cincinnati. He gave Rory money, told him to take Wendy out to a movie at the little theater on Main Street. He doesn't want the girl left alone. He knows how much she cries at night when she thinks he's asleep, and he knows sometimes the crying gets enough that she thinks she's gonna wake him. So she sneaks out of the one-room apartment they share and holes up in the bathroom, sobbing and smoking Pike's cigarettes in shuddering puffs. She's tough in the day, but misses her mother so much at night it makes Pike want to take a maul to his own bones.

Pike has no idea what to say to her. Just like her mother. And her mother's mother. She'd come from coal money, her whole life angling towards her education. Pike was just a senior year diversion, somebody to fuck around with on her way out of Nanticote. Then she got pregnant, and what with her mother being one of the pinch-mouthed local women, had to beg him for a place to stay.

Pike still can't think of a single good reason he had for agreeing. He knew better. And she sure as shit should have. Wasn't six months after Sarah was born before he started in on her. Shutting her eyes, blacking them into blood puddles in her head, beating on them until they were swollen closed, nothing but lumps of purple blood. Sarah screaming through every fight. Her mouth gaping like her jaw was swinging on a broken hinge, her eyes jumping around the room like horses leaping for the exit of a burning barn. But Alice never made a noise, just drug herself into the corner, letting Sarah do all the witnessing that needed done.

There are some things you can learn to live with. Most things you can't. Pike turns on the radio and Waylon Jennings is there, his voice rumbling through the cab like a surrogate engine. He lights a cigarette, thinking this is probably enough. That he shouldn't run this train of thought down, not right now. He knows better. These memories contain their own engines. You don't stop them until they're ready to be stopped.

Sarah's mother ended the fights, convincing Pike it was time to leave with the claw end of a hammer. She swung with both hands, all the way back from the shoulders like a baseball batter. Pike fingers the scars through his beard, smoking his cigarette, suddenly wishing very much that Alice were still alive. That he could have one last word with her.

CHAPTER 12

~ She said you were a real hard case. ~

Pike cruises Mulberry Street in slow motion, one hand draped over the steering wheel, his thin gray eyes scratching at the crumpled Over-the-Rhine street. The cracks yawning up out of the earth, through the foundations of the narrow Victorians. The small lawns wasted with broken glass and leaking garbage. The snow streaked yellow with piss. He passes a gang of boys standing on a corner, their hot black eyes sticking to him like tar. He drives another block, finds the address he's looking for.

His revolver in the glove compartment. A Ruger .357 with a four-inch barrel, standard but for the black walnut grips etched with eagles. Pike bought it in Juárez, thinking of weird John Brown. He slides it in his shoulder holster and steps down from the cab of his truck, booting the door shut with a bitter clank. It's the kind of neighborhood he's known well. There's only one reason you live in it if you're white. Meaning you always carry a gun. Pike steps out of the truck.

Number 400's a ruined brick pillar over the street. Just as he's about to knock, a reedy voice calls out, "there ain't nobody in there," and a prunish black woman steps off her stoop into her yard. She's wrapped in a tattered maroon housecoat, a filterless cigarette wisping smoke between her grisly fingers. "They're all gone. You looking for anybody in particular?"

"My daughter used to live here," Pike says.

"I'm Maude." The old woman slivers her cigarette between her thin lips, squints at him. "I've lived in this neighborhood for more'n seventy years. When'd she leave?"

"About a week ago."

"You mean little Wendy?" Maude cackles smoke. "I remember her fine, she used to come over to my house about every day and watch TV with me. I watched TV anyway. She read. Read near every book in my house."

Pike shakes his head. "I have Wendy. Sarah was my daughter."

The sky above them is gray and impenetrable, the thin winter clouds fused into the firmament and set like cement. Maude looks at it. "You already know?" she says.

"I already know."

Maude rolls her crimped cigarette in her fingers until the coal drops out and fizzles in the snow, then she stuffs the spent butt in her housecoat pocket. "Sarah used to talk about you. She said you were a real hard case."

"I was."

"How long since you'd seen her?"

"She was six."

"That's a long time. Did you have a reason?"

"I had a few good ones."

"Would you like a cup of coffee?"

"I have things that need to get done today."

"Do you?" Maude peers at him. "What is it you need to get done?"

"I need to see her grave. If you'll tell me where it is."

Maude chucks her head up the street. "Take a left at the first light, go on about a quarter of a mile. It'll be on your left, McCulloch Hill Cemetery. The curator'll tell you where to find her plot."

Pike turns to his truck.

"You come back sometime and I'll tell you why I had her buried there," Maude says after him. Although it isn't until he's already in the truck and driving away that he remembers her saying it.

CHAPTER 13

~ They reburied the one and carted the other off in crates. ~

It's a small cement marker, plugged into the frozen ground. There's no epitaph, only her name. Pike flips his spent cigarette into the snow and lights another, the gravestone darkening to inscrutable under a passing cloud, then lightening in the raspy winter sun. Dead tree branches knob up out of the snow like black fossilized elbows poking from under a white sheet, and the hill's littered with other gravestones that look exactly like Sarah's. Haphazard slabs, stuck crookedly in the hillside. Each a terse acknowledgement that someone who wouldn't be missed much died abruptly.

The curator, a septuagenarian with cheeks that cling like curtains around his crumbling teeth, had apologized for the condition of the grounds. He brought a broom out of his shack at the gate to sweep the snow off, explaining that not many people visited anymore. He discoursed on the graveyard's history while he swept. That it was found to be a Hopewell mound thirty years ago. That the city had buried people in it for over a century and it took the anthropologists ten years to separate the white corpses from the Indian corpses. That they reburied the one and carted the other off in crates. That they then reopened the graves for transients.

"Figured it needed restocking?" Pike asked.

The old man had chuckled. "That's about the long and the short of it."

A sputtering of snowflakes collects in Pike's hair and beard. He drops his cigarette and turns up the collar of his work jacket and lights another. It's good there aren't any visitors. If there were, he'd shorten his visit. He knows the image he makes against the grave-stones and the blanket of white snow. He couldn't stand being on display, paralyzed by the memory of a woman he barely knew, who had just happened be his daughter.

There ought to be an epitaph. Any epitaph. Pike dredges through his memory for one and comes as close as he can. "Here grow no damned drugs. Here are no storms," he says aloud. It's inadequate. He smokes his cigarette until there's nothing but a smoldering scrap of paper between his fingers, staring at the tombstone as though some kind of answer might bloom out of it.

None does. He doesn't even have a good question.

CHAPTER 14

~ I get lucky now and then. ~

Wendy walks the ditch towards town, cigarette smoke pluming out of her clothes with every brisk little step. Mostly it's Pike's. Its sunk into her the way it sinks into everything he comes in contact with. She's used to chemical smells, bitter aspirin smells, smells that wrack bodies and ruin minds, that consume and flatten people you love. She likes the smell of his tobacco smoke.

After the movie she and Rory had caught a ride with Iris to Rory's shack and she read to him while he worked out with his dumbbells. It took him two hours, moving from large muscles to small muscles with backbreaking precision, scar tissue grinding around his battered bones like shopwelded machine parts. She read him Poe and he liked the stories fine. It'd given her a little hope for him after all.

Wendy talks to herself while she walks. Mutters, more like, a non-sensical string of half formed words that pick at her until they pop compulsively out of her mouth. Her gloved hands clenching, smacking at each other, Monster squirming against her belly, mewling for mercy. She doesn't have a choice but to sputter and flail. There are words she has to throw away in hopes of not saying the ones she wants to most.

"Don't tell me you're walking all the way into town."

Wendy's eyes swing up like a pair of twin pistols. The creep from the bar, slushing along next to her in his black Monte Carlo. Jesus, she hadn't even noticed. "What the fuck do you want?" she snarls.

He grins the kind of grin that drops the temperature ten degrees. "It's a hell of a mouth you've got on you," he says.

Wendy's walking the left side of the road, his car idling alongside her in the oncoming lane. "You better get on your own side of the road," Wendy says.

"Why don't you hop in? I'll give you a ride."

"Ha! Why don't you suck a bullet, cocksucker?"

Derrick laughs out loud. "Who taught you to talk like that?"

"Here comes a truck," Wendy says. It's a full size pickup, coming around a bend in the road about an eighth of a mile ahead, barreling straight on at Derrick's Monte Carlo.

"He'll move," Derrick says nonchalantly.

"Maybe not. I get lucky now and then."

The truck blares its horn and swerves around the Monte Carlo, cutting and dragging a swathe of bitter winter air over Wendy. "I like this," she says. "Let's keep it up until that bend in the road yonder. Ain't nobody'll be able to see you coming around it."

"You're a hard case," he says. "You sure you don't want a ride?"

"No thanks, you fucking pervert. You fucking rapist."

A cream colored Cadillac slithers around the bend, narrowly dodges the Monte Carlo. The driver skipping the horn, signaling with his finger.

"Where are you coming from anyways?" he asks.

Wendy raises her eyes to the sky. "One semi truck, right now. Please."

"I remembered where I knowed you from."

Wendy snorts derision, keeps walking. "I think I'd remember if I knew you. Creepy pedophile shitlicker like you are." They're within fifty feet of the bend. Wendy thinks she hears a truck engine rumbling around it.

Derrick chuckles. "I doubt that, Wendy."

Her face shoots up at his like he's thrown ice water on her. But he's no longer there. He's gunned the gas and jerked the wheel, slipping into his own lane just in time, a blue Mack Granite hauling a load of coal waffling on the blacktop, the driver spinning the wheel to avoid him.

CHAPTER 15

~ They meet downtown, like a hammer and an anvil,
flattening everything between them in the process. ~

Derrick drives for three hours flat before he even realizes he's driving, pulling smoke out of a pack of Marlboros until the hair on his fingers crisps. Driving too fast, barely hanging onto the icy road. His brain hopping, skittering. He didn't remember who she was until he said her name. He dragged it out of some ditch in his memory he didn't even remember being there.

He's on I-75 now, five miles outside of Cincinnati on the Kentucky side. Whipping down the empty interstate and winging over the last Kentucky hill into the Ohio valley. The skyline unfurling and the Carew Tower rocketing over the city, its spotlights skimming up its base like ignition towards the already come and gone, and next to it, the pyramidal PNC building, a garish red and green sputtering like exhaust from its pillars. Below, the light from the lamps strung along the diagonal stays of the Roebling Suspension Bridge, muddying with the cacophony of multicolored beacons awash in the Ohio, blending so that the world tilts on its axis, so that the city lights drop around him like low hung stars. Then he's flying through them like through raindrops, careening across the trusses of the Brent Spence Bridge, curving away to the I-74 exit.

Cincinnati's hundreds of cities, thousands, but its inhabitants usually narrow it down to two. One of them the west side, the affluent side, rolling hills and quaint neighborhoods where police rookies pull guard duty on the demarcation lines. The other, the east side, the product of slaves and German immigrants and the hatred they've fostered between them. Cincinnati's cops live on the east side, Cincinnati's governors live on the west side. They meet downtown, like a hammer and an anvil, flattening everything between them in the process.

Derrick catches the Cheviot exit, cruises the burger joints and neighborhood bars, then spins the wheel down a side street, through a long stretch of two story Tudors. He sees the one he's looking for, checks the lit windows, pulls to the curb.

Klaus's wife answers the door, drying a cast iron skillet with a hand towel, her blonde hair pulled back in a severe bun. She doesn't smile at Derrick. East side German women never smile. It's rough work shouldering back the blacks, making sure they don't overrun your neighborhood. She chucks her chin at a footpath leading around back of their house. "Go around back. We don't need trouble."

Trouble. Derrick sure as hell feels like trouble. Around back, Klaus slides the glass door open with his elbow, carrying two beer bottles in one meaty hand, a thick cigar in the other. He's square-jawed, big, with a bushy black mustache that makes him look like a nineteenth century bare-knuckle boxer. He hands one of the beer bottles to Derrick. "I thought you'd split town."

"Just visiting."

"You caught me in time for a cigar." Klaus uses his forearm to clear snow off one of the deck chairs and sits, facing his dark yard. "Sit," he says, gesturing at the other deck chair, digging a pack of matches out of his breast pocket.

Derrick rocks on his heels, finishes half the beer in one ravenous gulp.

"I quit cigarettes for the kids, but I ain't quitting cigars." Klaus bends his face over a lit match, puffs the cigar to life. "I'll do anything for my kids twenty-three and a half hours a day. But I get a half an hour a day to sit out here and look at my yard." He looks fondly at the cigar and rotates it in his hand, blowing on the coal. "I take it you're after news?"

"Yep."

"Well, everybody's pulling for you. There ain't a cop in the city doesn't know what kind of piece of shit that nigger was. Even the chief wants it to die down, to get you back on."

"But?"

"But the one guy who should be in your corner is finding new ways to fuck you. You can't turn on the television without hearing him make some backhanded comment about your record, firing up the natives."

"Fleischer."

Klaus nods, his heavy cigar hand draped over one huge knee. "What'd you do to him anyway?"

"I found his daughter at her place of employment."

Klaus chuckles. "How'd you figure out who she was?"

"They get blotchy in the same places when they get excited."

Klaus guffaws cigar smoke. "So what're you gonna do now?"

Derrick sends his cigarette sparking into the blackness. "I'll figure something out." He sticks his hands in his pockets, stares densely out at nothing.

CHAPTER 16

~ Wendy's eyes fire familiarly in her head. ~

"Y
ou can't tell Pike," Wendy says. They sit on a bench on the courthouse lawn, huddled over steaming Styrofoam cups of coffee. Her face looks like a scrimshaw broach bundled in a black scarf, her lips blood red in the cold.

"Why?" Rory doesn't even want to think about holding out on Pike.

"Because I said so." She kicks at the snow. "I don't have a reason. I don't want him to know."

Rory winces as the coffee hits a loose tooth. He clears his throat. "I think I have to."

Wendy's eyes fire familiarly in her head.

Rory shrugs helplessly. "Say what you want, but he's as smart as they come. He'll know what to do."

"He'll make things worse," Wendy says. "He doesn't make any sense even when he wants to." She bites her lip. "You could talk to the creep yourself. You could find out what he wants."

Rory shakes his head. "He's scared of Pike. You could tell that by looking at him. He ain't scared of me."

Wendy hurtles her coffee. The top pops and the watery coffee spins in an arc over the lawn, steaming and browning the clean white snow. She stands up and snorts frost.

"Sorry, kid," Rory says after her.

CHAPTER 17

~ Without any of the strangled hatred that turned it all bad. ~

The gray sun gasps once, dies behind the Green Frog Café. Dark coming on. The truck's engine idling in rough snorts, the dashlights flickering an alien green. Pike spins the wheel on his .357, and thumbs it back into the frame. Then rests his thick arms on the steering wheel, the big revolver's muzzle draping down at the steering column. "I ain't sure I like this."

"It's a damn sight better than what you came up with," Rory says. "Cotton and him are friends. You walk in there and start pistol-whipping him, Cotton's liable to blow your head off."

Pike's eyes run down the cars in The Green Frog's gravel lot, rest on the black Monte Carlo parked next to the entrance. "Not likely."

Rory grins. "Someday you're gonna meet up with somebody that ain't impressed with you."

Pike lifts a Pall Mall out of the pack on his dashboard and lights it.

Rory opens the truck door, still grinning. "And when you do, I want to be there to see it."

Pike watches Rory's broad back sway towards the bar, running with a bloody current of muscle under his sweatshirt. There are times he reminds Pike of all the good things Pike was when he was Rory's age. Only about a hundred times better. And without any of the strangled hatred that turned it all bad.

CHAPTER 18

*~ Six hundred pounds of grisly fat, with slick
infantile faces and girlish pale blue eyes. ~*

"**C**otton ain't here," Leroy says, shifting a case of Budweiser long-necks into the cooler behind the bar.

Rory takes a stool. Derrick's sitting at a table across from two fat rednecks, holding a hand of cards. One of the rednecks is wearing a Bengals ball cap, the other a Reds cap, but other than that they're a duplicate six hundred pounds of grisly fat, with slick infantile faces and girlish blue eyes. They're locals. Identical twins, one named Jesse and the other Jessie, both after Elvis's stillborn twin brother. Their mother a bit on the liquor-addled side. "Guess I'll have a drink and wait until he shows up."

"He probably ain't gonna be in today." Leroy tips one of the long-necks at Rory. "And, anyway, you don't drink."

"I drink Coke."

"The only way I sell Coke is with bourbon in it. If you just want Coke, I gotta charge you for both."

"Just Coke."

Leroy shrugs and sprays out a Coke, then pours himself the bourbon. Rory sips his Coke and watches Leroy toss off the bourbon and get back to moving beer place to place. Rory doesn't try to strike up conversation with him. Talking while working ain't an option for the poor bastard.

Derrick, over his cards, " . . . he made her eat shit. I saw it crusted around her mouth when I was untying her."

Jesse, sorrowfully, clucking his tongue, "The poor child."

Jessie, enraged, "That's nigger work. You can't tell me anybody but a nigger would do a little girl like that."

Derrick, "I did him like a nigger, too. Tied him up with her ropes

57

and took my Buck knife to him. Cut around about a silver dollar out of the top of his head, dug an elbow in and gave his mangy afro a good yank. Took a whole nugget of his scalp right off. Then stuffed it in his mouth."

Jesse, remorsefully, "I can't imagine what that poor child must have endured."

Jessie, choked with hatred, "The coon got what he deserved. You should have tarred and feathered him, too. Set him on fire and strung him up from the highest tree."

Derrick, "Bet I'm the first man to scalp anybody in these parts for a long time, anyway."

Jesse, "I hope you didn't leave him in pain."

Jessie, "I hope he didn't leave that room alive."

Derrick's laugh is a raspy explosion, a chainsaw hitting rebar. "You two dumb motherfuckers say the same goddamn thing every time you open your mouths." There's a long silence, then the sound of Derrick patting his pockets down. Then, "I'll be damned, boys. Look who we got at the bar."

Rory relaxes his stiffening back by force of will.

A shuffle, a chair falling on all fours, footsteps. Then a hand on Rory's shoulder and Derrick's stinking bourbon breath. "Cotton ain't here, boy."

"I know it."

Derrick reaches over Rory's shoulder and drops a bill on the bar. "Bourbon," he says to Leroy. "And get him another one, on me."

Leroy pours Derrick's bourbon, then sprays out Rory's Coke.

"Coke?" Derrick's laugh shotguns out again. "You scared to drink liquor around me?"

Rory eyes Derrick's face in the mirror behind the bar. "I ain't scared of you."

"That's gonna be your mistake." Derrick's jagged jawline sets like its been hammered straight on an anvil. "There something you want to know about me, boy?"

"Yeah," Rory says. He watches Derrick's shoulders in the mirror, his own loose and ready to move. "Who the fuck are you?"

Derrick's good humor returns, dropping over his face like a

guillotine. He guffaws and slaps the bar. "Ain't you been hearing me talk? You want to know who I am, you just ask any nigger in Cincinnati."

CHAPTER 19

~ *Pike'd already have his .357 out, pistol whipping him*
until the skin hung off his face in bloody sheets. ~

I t snows during the night, all night. Pike dreams of Mexico. He always does. Days, he doesn't let himself think past the borders, nights he still has his room in Juárez over the bookseller's shop, with the flower box on the window and the bathroom that never has hot water and always smells of urine. He dreams of the hot dusty sun wavering over the city, the plumes of exhaust that roll off the street through his glassless window. He dreams of waking each morning without the weight of where he's from sitting on his chest like an animal.

There was a bar across the street that ebbed and flowed with the changing shifts at the GE maquiladora. It had a real name, but it has a different dream name every time Pike revisits it. In between runs for Joaquin, Pike spent his time in that bar, sitting, reading, drinking. The bartender was a thin gray man who spoke English and shared his books with Pike. Some nights they argued about them long after the bar closed.

Those were Pike's good nights. On his bad nights he crossed the border into El Paso, trolling the honkeytonks, scoring cocaine, settling in some dive where he could blow lines off the bar. Those nights he drank too much, his eyes smoking in their sockets, his greasy black hair whipping around his head. Then he ran out of coke, every time. So he wanted to fight, every time. He insulted the local shitkickers, and if one made the mistake of protesting, he drove his head into a wall. Sometimes one'd pull a knife, but he was always too slow. Pike'd already have his .357 out, pistol-whipping him until the skin hung off him face in bloody sheets. Those nights he woke in a ditch.

When Pike dreams of Mexico he always dreams of a girl. Tonight is no exception. Her name was Guillermina, and Pike dreams of a slow tourist train ride into the Sierra Madres where she never left his side. What a woman can talk you into. He dreams she's in the bed next to him still.

She's not. He wakes to the one-room apartment he shares with Wendy, lying alone on the pallet he's made himself on the floor. Snowflakes churn in the streetlights, the streetlamps splaying nickels of light through the frost on his window, over the floor and up the six-column radiator that sits against the wall, trickling runny heat out into the room.

Wendy's sleeping in his bed. She's barely spoken to him since seeing Derrick, as though she's found some connection between the two that she can't disentangle from her mother's death. Not that there's any doubt but she's right. The night before, they ate dinner at the Oxbow and Pike told her she'd be staying with Iris while he and Rory were in Cincinnati. She took it bad. Stood up from the booth, spat full in Rory's face, walked out without looking back. She was in bed when Pike came in.

He wants to raise himself up to look at her sleeping face, but he doesn't. Instead, he turns on the police scanner he keeps by his pallet and smokes cigarettes quietly, listening to dead air, watching the morning light split like a wound through his window.

She wakes finally, blinking her way into the cool morning air, her hand automatically roving over the threadbare quilt for Monster. His bony ribcage shudders and his eyes flutter open at her touch. He yawns sharp teeth and brushes his tongue across her hand.

Neither of them bothers to look at Pike.

BOOK II

It's a long ol' road that never ends
It's a long ol' road that never ends
It's a long ol' trail that never ends
It's a bad wind that never changes.

— Blind Lemon Jefferson

CHAPTER 20

~ *It makes it easier that way.* ~

The truck rocks and sways down the two-lane highway like a sick lion running down an antelope. Pike sits with one hand on the wheel, the other smoothing down his beard. "How'd you know Derrick, anyway?" he asks.

Rory doesn't look at him. "Seen him at the Green Frog."

"I never seen you drink."

"I don't. I go there to see Cotton."

Pike cracks his window, lights a Pall Mall with his Zippo. Snaps it shut. "That part of your plan to become a boxer?"

"Maybe. Sometimes. Probably not."

It makes you heavy all over just thinking about being Rory's age. "Try to remember there are other things in the world but fighting."

"I know it."

"Just in case it doesn't work out."

Rory stares out the window over one of his fists. "The Toughman contest coming up. That's it. Then if I'm done, I'm done. I'll be the best carpenter you ever saw."

"Koreans call it bone rank," Pike says. "That's the difference between those who can and those who can't. You don't get where you are by pulling yourself up by your bootstraps, it's something built into your bones. It makes it easier that way. You understand?"

"Not a word."

Pike sticks the tip of his cigarette out of the window and lets the winter air whip the ashes off it. "Just this. I never knew anyone who fucked up their life good who didn't think they were special. The holes they dug themselves into were exactly the shape of their dreams."

"That the wisdom you brought back from your years on the road?"

"You are what you are. The best way to fuck up your life good is to try to be something else."

"Let's leave it alone." Rory sucks air through his fist. "Why don't you tell me what we're supposed to be doing instead?"

"Krieger says he knows Wendy. I want to know from where." Pike uses his index finger to resettle his glasses on his nose. "I'm guessing it was through her mother. I figure if I run down enough people who knew Wendy's mother, sooner or later I'll find the connection."

"Did you know her well enough to do that? I never even knew you had a daughter until Wendy showed up."

"I barely knew her at all. I'll pay you the same as I pay you at work. And you can quit anytime. No hard feelings. Say the word and I'll have you on the next bus out of Cincinnati."

"I told you last night I'm in. Always do sober what you said you'd do drunk. That'll teach you to keep your damn mouth shut."

Pike looks at him, cigarette smoke wafting out of his beard as if exhaled by the pores in his face.

"That's a Hemingway quote." Rory grins. "I got it from Wendy. It kind of fits, don't it, even if I wasn't drunk?"

CHAPTER 21

~ Niggertown. ~

"Hell of a neighborhood," Rory says, watching a scabrous dog sniff at a shitstained patch of snow under a long row of disintegrating brick homes, each of them leaning precariously at a different dilapidated angle.

"Niggertown." Pike feeds a cigarette butt through his cracked window.

Rory winces. "I just meant it looks kind of rough. Like there's some drug action, for sure."

"Niggertown," Pike repeats, as if they were again saying the same thing. "Pop the glove box."

Rory swings the lid down with a clank. "Think we need them?" he asks, eyeing the compartment.

"Give me the big one," Pike says, "the one underneath is yours."

Rory hands Pike the stainless steel .357, holding it by the barrel like it's something distasteful. Pike takes it by the grip and wipes the barrel on his jeans to take off Rory's fingerprints, then slides it in his shoulder holster. "Take yours."

Rory pulls a Glock 19 out of the glove compartment. He cradles it in both hands, holstered.

"You know how to use it?"

Rory shakes his head.

Pike takes the pistol from him and shakes the holster off. He jacks the slide, reholsters it, hands it back to Rory. "You pull the thing that sticks out on the bottom. We call it a trigger."

Rory loosens his belt with one hand. The gun's heavier than he thinks it should be. Strange, square, cumbersome, he can't seem to hold it any way that isn't awkward. He threads the holster through his belt, smoothes his sweatshirt over the bulge. "I'm not sure a gun's the way I want to go."

"Then don't pull it. But it's a damn sight better to have it and not need it, than the other way around."

CHAPTER 22

~ Her eyes like black nailheads hammered
into hard black wood. ~

Maude opens the door wearing a frayed purple housecoat, looking smaller, more shriveled in, like a pomegranate going old. "Well," she says, "you must have known I was making coffee."

"I've got questions," Pike says.

"Come on in." She turns and shuffles creakily down the dimly lit entrance hall towards the bright kitchen at the end. Pike follows, stepping around the stacks of books that line the hallway. There are hundreds of them, angled up the walls in reckless piles. Everything from leatherbound tomes on the settling of Kentucky to paperback bestsellers with titles like *Dead Yellow Women*. Rory tiptoes behind him like he's scared to disturb the air, like any foreign current might start the books dominoing to the floor. Then they're in the kitchen. The floor tiled white with green, the green walls paled with nicotine.

"Sit down," Maude says, gesturing at the vinyl-topped kitchen table. They do. She fumbles three mugs out of a cabinet and pours coffee out of a steel stovetop coffee maker, then sinks into a chair, letting out a hoarse sigh. She breathes heavily for a minute or two before she asks, "cream or sugar?"

"Don't trouble yourself," Pike says, and he means it. He ain't entirely sure she'd survive having to stand up again. "Black's fine."

"For me too," Rory says, taking up his cup. "Thank you, ma'am,"

"You're welcome." She eyes him. "What's your name, boy?"

"Rory, ma'am."

"Ma'am, he says." She chuckles. "Were you in the military?"

"No, ma'am. Just habit."

Maude flicks her eyes over at Pike. "Not one you picked up from him, I'll bet."

"No, ma'am," Rory says, grinning, "not from him. From my dad. He always told me it didn't cost nothing to be polite."

"I've got questions," Pike says.

"You said that."

"I'm looking for a girl named Dana. Sarah used to run around with her."

Maude pulls the long stub of a Camel out of a heavy glass ashtray filled with long stubs and shakes her head. "I never learned much about Sarah's friends."

"She was a hooker," Pike says, as though that might jog her memory. "Same as Sarah." He sees Rory start.

Maude nods, sparking a kitchen match on the chrome edge of the table and lighting her cigarette. "I figured that. But Sarah and I traveled in different circles."

Pike watches her wrinkled face tighten and warp around her cigarette. She watches him back, her eyes like black nailheads hammered into black wood. "How about a man named Krieger?" he tries, "Derrick Krieger?"

"Derrick Krieger?" Maude blows smoke at the ceiling. "What in God's name are y'all looking for him for?"

Pike doesn't know well enough what he'd be lying about to bother. "He says he knows Wendy."

"Well. Don't let him get ahold of her."

Rory's tan forehead wrinkles in confusion and his eyes flit from Maude to Pike, then back. "How come you know Krieger?" he asks.

"Krieger's the policeman that caused the riots." She looks at their blank faces for a long minute. Then for another like they might be fooling her. Then she shrugs. "I guess it ain't news everywhere. He was setting a boy up for a drug bust and when the boy figured out he was being set up, he ran. Krieger shot him twice in the back. Then once more in the head, so close it set his hair on fire. You couldn't leave your house for almost a week. He's on leave while the department investigates. Him and his partner."

"What's his partner's name?" Pike asks.

"I don't know anything about that. The papers barely bother with him."

Pike smoothes down his beard, thinking.

Maude eyes him, letting smoke drift out of her wizened nose. "That what you were looking for?"

"Partly." Pike nods for a minute. "I think I owe you thanks," he begins again slowly. "Last time I saw you, you told me to come back and you'd tell me why you buried my daughter."

"You don't owe me nothing," Maude says. "I didn't really bury your daughter, I just told the folks from the county where to do it. That's what I told you. To come back and I'd tell you why I had her buried her where I had her buried."

Pike looks at her.

"Cincinnati's an old city, Mr. Pike, older than most people know. It was founded by a band of ex-slaves, poor whites and Indians. They called themselves the Ben Ishmael Tribe. They were wandering tinkers and minstrels, and Cincinnati was one of the stops on their route. It was only after they'd cleared the land for themselves that the white settlers moved in to claim it. Did you know that?"

"There's a whole pile of things I don't know," Pike says.

Maude doesn't look surprised. "They used to caravan between here and Indianapolis. Even after Cincinnati was civilized they still used it as a stopping point, but they were made to camp down on the shore of the Ohio with the boatmen and the dockworkers. My grandfather used to take his pots down to their camp for mending. He said there was everything in the world down there. The dirty rich smell of the plants the Indians and Africans burnt to keep themselves clean, the creeping sound of Scotch Irish fiddles, the dirge-like cant of the Muslims intoning back to Mecca, everything. He said they kept fires burning, too, all around the edge of the camp. Fires burning with some kind of grimy wood smeared in pitch. He said walking through that greasy smoke was like walking into some other world. Time ran backwards when you stepped into that smoke."

"They still around?" Rory asks.

She shakes her head. "That was at the beginning of the century, and there was plenty of talk about putting mongrel races out of existence.

As I read, they were penned up in roughcut forts on the bank of the Ohio and army doctors were sent in to hack out the women's uteruses."

"A nation only regenerates itself on a heap of corpses," Pike says.

"Saint Just," Maude says.

Pike raises his eyebrows.

"I'd forgot about them for years. But I was reading a book on them when Sarah died. And I remembered how she showed up in Over-the-Rhine like she had some kind of claim on it. She had a Scotch Irish fiddle she played, too. So when the men came to take her body I asked them to bury her on McCulloch Hill. With the way names get set on things around here, I figured it had to have something to do with the Ishmael tribe." She shrugs. "It was a whim."

"I didn't know she played the fiddle," Pike says.

"She used to say it reminded her of you." Maude looks at him. "But then most things in her mind circled back to you if you followed them long enough."

Rory rocks back and forth on the hind legs of his chair, off somewhere else completely. "How come I never heard of them? The Ben Ishmaels."

"Places swallow stories," Maude says. "Especially stories that nail it down as what it doesn't want to be."

"You said you never saw Krieger coming around," Pike says. "Do you know anybody who might have? Anybody in the neighborhood who might've kept an eye out?"

Maude sticks a fresh cigarette in her mouth and fingers a piece of tobacco off her lips and wipes it on the rim of the ashtray. "You might try those two boys who live in the house on the other side of hers. Number 402, I think. They look to be a little of her type."

Pike raps the table twice and stands abruptly. "Thank you." When she starts to rise to show them the door, he raises his hand for her to stay seated. "We can find our own way out."

CHAPTER 23

~ Whatever they'd been doing to the poor
bitch, they'd been doing it a long time. ~

Number 402's brick is going green with mold and the lopsided porch rambles away from its pillars, one corner of it propped up with cement blocks. A tattered chain link dog kennel runs down the side, the cement floor smeared all over with fresh dog shit and dirt. Pike raps three times on the door.

"What do you make of her story?" Rory asks. "About the Ben Ishmaels?"

"You stick your arm into any of these local histories, you'll come out shit up to your elbow."

"I could tell you didn't think much of it."

"It was her using my daughter as a bookmark I didn't think much of." Pike raps on the door again to no more response than he got the first time. He thumbs his glasses up his nose and unholsters his .357.

"We're starting with the guns out?"

Pike holds a hand up for him to be silent. Movement inside. A scuffle, a crash and the quick harsh rasp of a dog barking. Pike rears back and kicks the door in.

"Should've figured that was coming," Rory says.

The house is a double of Maude's. Pike takes the dingy hallway in three strides. Rory follows, kicking through mounds of garbage, fumbling the Glock clear of his pants. A huge bald man huddles in a wheelchair at the kitchen table, his eyes wobbling in his head like bulbs of fat. Next to him, a kid with a wispy blonde goatee scratches through a pile of cigarette packs and Black Label cans. Pike plants the muzzle of his .357 about two inches from the kid's head, but he keeps scrabbling through the trash, oblivious, his brow furrowed in concentration. Then he finds what he's looking for and spins, holding an electric stun gun at Pike, electricity arcing blue between the metal prongs.

Pike thumbs the .357's hammer back, unimpressed.

"I'd drop it," Rory says. "He's been looking for somebody to shoot all day." The stun gun clatters on the tile floor and Rory winks at the kid. "Good choice."

"What do y'all want with us?" The kid's wearing faded blue jeans and a filthy white T-shirt with the sleeves cut off. "We ain't got nothing to rob."

"Nothing?" Pike picks a syringe off the table and tosses it on the floor.

"We ain't got none left."

"We ain't here for your smack." Pike raps the kid's forehead with the muzzle of his gun. "We're here to talk." He cracks the kid on the forehead again, raising a welt. "Now."

The kid throws his hands up between the gun and his face. "Jesus, man," he squawks. "What the fuck do you want to talk about?"

"Start with your name."

"Bogey."

"Suits you." Pike flicks his eyes at the idiot. His wheelchair fidgets back and forth in short jerks and a spit bubble wavers on his mouth like a water puddle in an earthquake. "You?"

"His name's Wood," Bogey says. "He don't talk."

Wood nods his fat head violently, the fat under his chin jiggling like pudding.

"Where's the dog?" Pike asks.

"Dog?" Bogey says innocently.

Pike barrel-raps him on top of the head again, spotting the welt with blood. "Jesus!" Bogey shrieks and points across the kitchen. "She's right there."

Pike looks. Rory looks. The room stands still.

She's a smallish black pit bull, a year or so from being a pup. She cowers in a narrow alley between the refrigerator and the grease-crusted stove, whimpering and rasping at the air with her tongue. One of her front legs is twisted impossibly back and she's bleeding from a ragged gash on top of her head, the floor around her layered with dog blood and shit. Whatever they've been doing to the poor bitch, they've been doing it a long time.

Rory tosses his Glock into his left hand and slaps Wood across the face with a hard right palm. Wood's head rollicks furiously on his fat plug of a torso and tears spring into his eyes.

Pike flashes him an appreciative grin. "You're picking up on this."

Rory stares Wood in the face. Wood snuffles and chokes, trying to hold back his tears, but he can't. His jaw drops, his eyes squint shut and he cuts loose with a long wet wail. Rory reaches back to let him have another palm.

"Hold up," Bogey screams hysterically. "Hold up."

Rory looks at him.

"That ain't right. He ain't but a kid, man. Up here." Bogie taps his temple. "He's retarded. He don't know no better."

Rory turns to him. "You do?"

"Hey, man, we was only having fun." Bogie's face is pinched and cringing. "No big deal."

"Let's see it."

"All right, man." Bogie shuffles on the floor for the stun gun, his eyes fixed on Rory. "Watch the dog," he says, and crawls to her on all fours through the shit and the blood. Rory watches the dog. Bogie punches a button and jams the probes into the dog's ribs.

Her jaw gapes and her head vibrates, flinging dog blood and spit in stringy arcs across the kitchen. Her eyes roll in her sockets, her broken paws pound an electrified tap dance on the kitchen tile. Wood's round face explodes in a huge smile and he bangs on the arm of his wheelchair, erupting in a high-pitched screech of joy.

Bogie pulls the stun gun back. The dog collapses on the floor like her bones have disintegrated under her skin. "See, it ain't no big deal." Bogies stands and his eyes flinch up at Rory's hand. "I kind of think she likes it."

Rory swallows thickly and his gun hand drops limply to his side, the way a man run through in a duel might drop his sword.

"You knew my daughter." Pike's voice is low and level. "Her name was Sarah, and we know you knew her."

Bogie scratches the back of his head. "No, I don't believe I do."

Pike swings his .357 on the dog and pulls the trigger. The muzzle blast haloes his fist in fire and the bitch's head sprays blood vapor and bone chunks. Woods shrieks wildly and smacks at his ears as though the boom of the handgun is an insect swarm he can slap away. Pike levels the .357 at his chest. "Your friend's next," he says to Bogie. "Then you. I'm looking forward to you."

Bogie's chin bobs up and down frantically. "She was a hooker. Used to live across the street. We had some of the same friends. She come over a couple times and partied with us. She's dead now."

"What else?"

"Nothing else. I barely knew her."

"You said you had mutual friends. Who?"

"Bitch named Dana."

"I know Dana. Where do we find her?"

Bogie hesitates, weighing his answer. Rory takes the stun gun out of his hand. He turns it over and finds the power button. "Hey, man," Bogie says, eyeing him. "There ain't no need for that. I'll tell you whatever you want to know."

Rory grabs the top of Bogie's head in one hand and rams the probes against his throat with the other, crushing in his windpipe. "I know where her mom lives," Bogie coughs out. "We broke in once, stole her TV. I can take you there."

Pike holsters his .357 and pulls a cigarette out of his pocket. He lights it with his brass lighter and snaps his lighter shut. Then nods at Rory.

Rory punches the power button. Bogie's head lurches forward, then back. The tendons in his neck hop and squirm to the tune of the juice and he tries to scream, but he can't. He gurgles on his saliva for a second or two. Then collapses on the shit-covered floor, pawing his neck and coughing, his face the color of a bruise.

"You're coming with us to Dana's mother's," Pike says. "If she ain't there I'm gonna shoot you in the face and dump you in a ditch."

Bogie hacks at the saliva in his windpipe, his face blotched all over with vicious red patches and all sickly white underneath. He tries to talk, can't.

"You understand?" Pike kicks him in the ribs with the point of his cowboy boot. Not lightly.

Bogie yelps and claws his side. "I can't leave Woods. He can't take care of himself."

"Sure he can." Pike boots the dog's food bowl across the room. It knocks up against Wood's wheelchair, sloshing runny shitlike dog food onto the floor. "Some food for you, you dumb motherfucker."

Wood's big face splits with sobs like a canvas awning splitting under the weight of a rainstorm.

CHAPTER 24

~ You can get away from a good upraising. ~

Derrick parks on the side of the mountain road on a turn-around overlooking Nanticonte. Devil's Elbow, they call the spot, but Derrick doesn't know why. It's where he comes to think. Always has been, ever since he was old enough to drive. He gets out and leans on the car and looks down on the small town, the town's buildings little more than darkened smudges in the swirling snow and the coal smoke, the power cables drawing out into the mountains like a map grid, and then lost in the trees, as though looking at an old photograph. He cracks a beer and drinks. The town looks to have been stuck down in these mountains since the mountains got stuck here, to have become a part of the landscape. And it has, in a way. Nothing changes. Fifteen years from the end of the twentieth century, but you sure as hell can't tell it here. The women with their hive hairdos, the men with their buzzcuts, the kids growing theirs long, wearing Rolling Stones shirts, smoking reefer.

You can get so far away from where you're from you can't ever come back. Not entirely. You can break all ties with your past, you only have to be willing to carve a chunk out of yourself you won't mind missing the rest of your life. And you have to be ready to deal with whatever kind of shit the holes'll fill up with. The old lady long dead now, and the old man in a home, struck stupid with senility. Drooling and shitting on himself, completely shed of the only thing he ever had to brag about, his son the war hero. Derrick finishes his beer, tosses the can in the ditch. He was a good father. Well. You can get away from a good upraising. You can get away from most anything if you work at it hard enough.

Derrick reaches through the side window of the Monte Carlo to break out another beer. Half drunk already. What now? Buy a little house in this shithole town and settle down? Get fat on beer until the heart gives out altogether?

Well, why not?

He opens the beer and looks out on the town and spits. Then closes his eyes, as if exhausted from the exertion.

CHAPTER 25

~ Like some kind of apes crawling out of the mud. ~

Pike's smelled a few things in his life he could've gone without smelling. Shithouses in August, busted refrigerators full of meat, junkies with a year-long skim of filth on their skin to keep the heroin from escaping through their pores. And a roomful of broiled Mexicans, stuffed together and decaying, the stench rising like a great filthy bear and wrapping Pike in its greasy paws. He doesn't like to think of that one, and anyway, stuffed into the cab of his truck with Bogie anything you try to think gets run out of your mind by the stench. Pike lights a cigarette and tries to burn it out by inhaling the smoke through his mouth and nose at the same time. It doesn't work. He turns on the radio as if that might help.

"Nice place you had there," Rory says to Bogie, rolling down the window.

"Shit, it ain't mine," Bogie says. "That's all Woods. I'm just nursing the motherfucker 'cause his daughter's off getting married."

"Bet she'll be impressed with the job you're doing too."

"Hey, I take care of the motherfucker. Anyway, I got my own problems. I got a place on the West side. Got a woman, too."

"And she let you go to take care of your friend? Being the loving type you are."

"Shit, I'm loving. I keep her grass trim. Keep her lawn wet."

Rory looks at him.

"I plow her land. I know how to clean out her backyard."

"One more," Rory says, "and I'll shoot you." Pike thinks he's joking until he sees Rory's hand on the Glock.

Bogie doesn't notice. "Yeah, sure. Anyway, she set my trunk outdoors a couple weeks ago." His voice turns woeful. "Her family put her up to it. Bunch of backwards hillbilly motherfuckers. They don't like me being with her neither, saying I ain't good enough. Ain't that some shit? Bunch of shitass rednecks straight out of the hollow like some kind of apes crawling out of the mud. And I ain't good enough."

"Hard to see what they might have against you," Pike says.

"Fuck you. Anyway, one of them cocksuckers, her brother, came up on me, started talking shit about this and that and how I wasn't fit for his sister. Pissed me off, so I knocked about half his teeth out with a length of pipe. She got all salty over it. Said me being around wasn't good for the kids. I ain't seen none of them for almost a month." His eyes water and he puts his hand up to them. "Shit," he says. "I hate crying in front of motherfuckers."

"How many kids you got?" Rory asks.

"Two. Girls. I'm telling you, I can't live without them. When I'm asleep I'm dreaming about them. When I'm awake I get no rest."

"Get a job," Pike says. "Clean up."

Bogie shakes his head mournfully. "I got habits, man. There ain't no getting away from it. I can only be what I am. If I could be something else I would."

"Well, it's a hard row to hoe," Rory says.

"It is that. Sixty miles through rock, forty more through sand."

"Whyn't you two shut the fuck up before I start crying?" Pike says.

Bogie clutches his stomach and farts loudly, filling the cab with a sick rumble. "I been drinking beer all day. I need food," he whines.

Rory sticks his whole head out the window, his Adam's apple spasming. Pike brakes the truck at a cross street. "Which way?"

"Left. Then take a right at the light. Dana's old lady lives over in Hyde Park, we got a ways to go." Bogie's stomach makes a sound like a bull elephant being garroted. "I was so hungry once I ate a robin." He farts again. "Oh Jesus."

"Please stop," Rory croaks.

Pike wheels the truck into a restaurant parking lot. The building's whitewashed and stained all over with black snow-water and dirt. The sign says Bar & Grill, nothing else. "One burger," Pike says. "But I swear to God, if you fart one more time I'll beat you to death with my bare hands."

CHAPTER 26

~ Like I ain't fit to eat with normal folks? ~

The door rings open into a dark, dingy, windowless room with no grill to be seen. Nor customers. Behind the bar, a bone-thin, balding and bespectacled bartender in a Motley Crue T-shirt watches them. "You got any food?" Pike says.

"We got food." He nods at a door at the back of the bar. "Got three Mexicans in the kitchen."

"We don't eat Mexicans."

The bartender looks at him. "They do the cooking. That's what I meant."

"Well, give me three burgers. And some fries. Can I get it to go?"

The bartender's writing his order down. He looks up. "Sure."

Pike turns to Rory. "Take this little fucker to the bathroom and don't let him out until he's clean."

"I'm right here," Bogie says. "You ain't got to talk about me in the third person. Motherfucker."

Rory grips him by the back of his neck and shoves him down the bar towards the sign at the back of the bar. "Them bathrooms are for customers only," the bartender says in a creaky voice, peering at Pike over his hooknose, his eyes watery behind his glasses.

Pike drops a bill on the counter. "One of the burgers is his."

The bartender purses his lips and picks up the bill. "I'll tell the Mexicans to get on your order."

"Fine. You got a payphone?"

The bartender returns Pike's change, his lips squirming like night-crawlers in the hot sun. "Outside the front door."

Pike steps outside and stands in front of the pay phone. He stands for a minute, lighting a cigarette and watching traffic waffle through the dirty snow. Then he rolls his shoulders and grins a lean grin, the cigarette smoke playing in the winter wind, rising like a dissipating halo over his head. He picks up the pay phone and dials. A one-eared cat slinks around the side of the restaurant and sidles up to Pike, mewling. Pike gives it the toe of his cowboy boot.

"Yeah?" Jack answers.

"This is Pike."

"Where the hell you been, Pike? I was out at the job site."

"Cincinnati. We're taking the week off."

"What's in Cincinnati?"

The cat tries again. Persistency being one of the few virtues Pike admires, he hunkers down and scratches it between the ears. "You might be able to help me answer that."

"How so?"

"I'm looking for a cop. I know the name of his partner. Derrick Krieger."

"The Derrick Krieger that's moved in over at Cotton's place? After shooting that black boy up there?"

Pike had been hoping Jack might know a little less. "That's my boy."

"What are you getting yourself into?"

"Nothing I can very much help."

"Is it about Wendy?"

Pike lets his lungs empty of smoke. "Yep."

"I don't suppose you're gonna tell me about it?"

"You don't want me to. Not yet, at least."

Pause. "It may take me a little while. You got a number where I can reach you?"

"I'll call you tomorrow morning."

Jack hangs up.

Pike stands and grinds his cigarette out under the heel of his boot, the cat mewling. He opens the door just as Bogie returns from the bathroom, the scum skimmed out of his whiskers and a good portion of the dogshit and blood troweled off his jeans and wet down.

The bartender looks at Bogie. Then looks down at the bar. Then looks at Bogie again. Then he deliberately opens the waist-high door in the bar and walks steadily to the bathroom door.

"Motherfucker," Bogie says, watching his back. "I oughtta spit in your mouth."

Rory slaps him on the back of the head. "Shut up."

The bartender opens the bathroom door and stands there. Very still. For a very long time.

Then he closes the door, his lips mottled red and white with disgust. "Joseph," he calls.

A Mexican kid with a black eyes and a long ponytail sticks his head out of a dingy door next to the bathrooms.

"This bathroom's gonna need to be cleaned up."

"Fuck you," Bogie says.

The bartender looks at him blankly.

"You heard me," Bogie says. "You gotta come back in here and tell everyone how bad the bathroom needs cleaning after I use it? Like I'm some kind of dirty motherfucker? Like I ain't fit to eat with normal folks?"

"Joseph, call the police," the bartender says.

Joseph's got one foot and a mop bucket through the door. He sets the bucket down tiredly and turns around. Bogie leaps at the bartender and whistles a wild roundhouse right crunching into his nose. "Call the police!" the bartender trills, his voice cracking.

Rory moves to grab Bogie, but Pike drops a forearm across his chest, staying him. Bogie sinks another wild right into the bartender's nose, then kicks his spindly legs out from under him and jumps on his chest, jamming his fists into his face. Pike lights another cigarette, his gray eyes wrinkled with a smile that has yet to reach his mouth. Joseph had already reached the bathroom. He sighs and turns around and walks very slowly back towards the door to the kitchen. Another Mexican kid passes him, and without even looking at the tangle of fists and spittle-laced blood that is the bartender and Bogie, holds a greasy paper bag of food to Pike. "Gracias," Pike says, and takes it.

"Llamé a policía," Joseph calls out from the kitchen. "Estarán aquí pronto."

Pike lifts Bogie bodily off the bartender and carries him out the door, flailing and spitting like an enraged kitten.

CHAPTER 27

~ I'm looking for somebody that might convince me of it. ~

Dana's mother's house is a white Victorian trimmed in blue, with a golden weathercock atop its tallest spire and a welcome mat that looks suspiciously unused. It's the same immaculately maintained house as every other house on the street. Even the snow seems cleaner on this side of town. Pike thumbs his glasses up his nose, bangs the cold brass knocker on the door. After a minute, the door cracks against the security chain and a brown eye appears, made monstrous by a pair of chunky glasses. "What do you want?" a woman's voice scrapes out.

"I need to speak with Dana. She's a friend of my daughter."

The door slams shut.

"I can wait," Pike says to the door. "As long as I need to. And sooner or later the neighbors will wonder who the hell I am. They'll definitely wonder about the two I brung with me."

The door cracks again and the eye reappears, gazing over Pike's shoulder at the truck. Rory's lounged back in his seat, his face still beat purple and yellow from the last fight night, his muddy boots up on the dash. Bogie's reenacting his tussle with the bartender, screaming, spitting, his fists flying. Rory can't take anymore, draws a baggie of pills out of his sweatshirt pocket and palms a handful of them into his mouth.

Pike lights a Pall Mall, smiles kindly at her. "Wouldn't want my neighbors seeing them outside of my house."

The door creaks open slowly. She's holding a cigarette in an ivory cigarette holder, her face narrow and tapered, like a thin wedge she's spent her whole life trying to insert into other peoples' lives. "Dana's not here."

"Then I'll talk to you."

She doesn't make any attempt to hide her irritation. "You have five minutes." She turns and Pike follows her in.

It's the kind of living room setup upper middle class women buy on a payment plan to prove they're upper middle class. Wallpapered in gold gilt and cream and stuffed with matching furniture, the cherry varnished end tables stacked with photographs of poodles, dozens of them. Somewhere buried in the poodles, a glimpse of a much younger Dana. "You compete?" Pike asks.

The woman sits gingerly in a high-backed chair that matches the couch. "We are two toys and a standard, and we have each won ribbons this year." She looks at Pike like he's an insect that's narrowly escaped squashing and isn't worth a second try. "Mr.?"

"Pike."

"Mr. Pike, you don't look like the sort who's particularly interested in poodles."

"Just being friendly," Pike answers. "Mrs.?"

"Jennings." She cocks her head at him and peers through her thick glasses. "But you should know that, if your daughter was a friend of Dana's."

"My daughter and I weren't close."

"Ah." Mrs. Jennings grinds her cigarette out in a gold-flecked glass ashtray on the coffee table, affixes a new one in her holder. "Is your daughter in the same profession as mine?"

"As of last week she ain't. She's dead."

The woman's eyebrows arch unsympathetically. "My condolences."

"She's been working at it a long time."

"So what is it you want from Dana?"

"Sarah's death was ruled an overdose. I'm looking for somebody that might convince me of it."

"Aha," she says. "You know, when Dana began her run of terror I used to lie awake nights, looking for somebody to blame her behavior on. Of course, there was no one. She was never molested. Her father never touched her. And I never abused her or mistreated her in any way. Of course." She blows a thin cord of smoke towards the ceiling. "She is what she is. When she dies, it will be a death resulting from what she was. Do you understand?"

"When did you see her last?"

The woman sweeps her cigarette over brittle breastbone. "She was here a week or so ago. She was sober, briefly, and swore to remain so. I let her spend the night, then caught her rifling through my purse in the morning. I threw her out."

"Did she seem like she was in trouble? Spooked?"

"She seemed more anxious than normal, but truly, I have no idea. Whatever she is these days it's not anything I recognize. Nor anything I want to."

"You have a spare picture of her? I'm gonna need to find her."

Mrs. Jennings sticks her hand into the stack of poodle pictures and pulls out the photograph of her daughter. She hands it to Pike. "Keep it."

Pike slides the picture out of the frame and slips it in his breast pocket without looking at it. "You said she stayed here recently. Where?"

"She has a room upstairs."

"Any chance I could see it?"

She snorts.

Pike nods. "And you have no idea at all where she might be?"

"She's a junky and a whore, Mr. Pike. She's wherever you find junkies and whores." She stands to see him out, her gargantuan eyes wavering in the cigarette smoke like a heat mirage. "I don't happen to know where that is, nor do I care."

CHAPTER 28

~ Not without compensation. ~

There's a hint of smoke behind Pike's eyes as he come out of the house, like the bare beginning of a fire a hundred miles back in a thick Appalachian forest. He stands outside the truck and lights a cigarette as if to draw off some of his own heat, then swings into the driver's seat and turns on the radio.

"Can we please please listen to something besides country music?" Bogies whines. "Fucking please?"

"No," Pike says.

"Please? Goddamn I hate this shit. Stories about losers. I wanna hear a song about a motherfucker who gets the girl. Who doesn't fuck up his life."

"Wouldn't ring true to you anyhow," says Rory.

"Fuck you. Like this shit rings true. Fucking Pancho and Lefty. Outlaws. This shit ain't true."

"Sure it is. And you're living it, outlaw."

"Fuck you."

They hit a stoplight next to an East side wine store. A couple exits the store, the man in loafers, holding a bottle, his mate in high heels, walking crablike, giggling in his ear. Both of them afternoon tipsy, taking the bottle somewhere they can be alone together. The man catches Pike's eyes and stiffens, sobering visibly. He takes the woman by her arm, leads her at an increased pace down the sidewalk.

The light changes and Pike hits the gas. Rory clears his throat. "So what'd we find out?" he asks.

"We found out she's a junky," Pike says. "We found out she's a whore. Two bits of information we pretty much had nailed." Bogie chortles from between them. "What's funny?" Pike says, in a voice that tugs Rory's breath in.

"Junky whores ain't hard to find," Bogie says. "I know all about them."

"I figured that. Consider yourself drafted."

Bogie crosses his arms. "Not without compensation, I ain't."

Something black and malignant passes over Pike's brow.

"I mean it. I ain't no nigger. I don't work for free."

Pike's hand twitches like it has a mind of its own and Rory tenses, but he only reaches for his cigarettes in his breast pocket. "I'll give you twenty bucks a day."

"And necessaries. I need my necessaries, too." Bogie sets his jaw imperiously. "Y'all can start right now."

CHAPTER 29

~ It makes you want to claw at the sidewalks. ~

Pike follows Bogie's instructions, brings the truck to rest on the corner of a downtown side street off Main. The sun's crawled over the city horizon, leaving a grayish coating of light behind it like a slug's trail. Rory rolls down his window to get a better look at the city and the winter wind slashes ravenously into the cab.

"That hotel right there." Bogie points down Main at a six-story redbrick with huge bay windows and a front door that could serve a barn. It's the kind of hotel that had once spelled out luxury to the street below, but not anymore. Now the window ledges wander in crumbling slope and the brick's crusted with mold and pigeon shit. Now the Fort Washington sign in dirty yellow plastic reads only that there's no better times coming.

Bogie pops the door open and scoots out of the truck heading for the hotel, then stops when Pike and Rory follow his lead. "Well, goddamn it," Bogie says to them. "Ain't no one gonna sell to me with you two country peckerwoods hanging around."

"Not my problem," Pike says. "I sure as hell ain't handing you my money and letting you walk away."

Bogie shakes his head mournfully, starts towards the hotel's front entrance.

Rory sticks his hands in the front pockets of his sweatshirt and follows, head hunched down. Even as cold as it is, there are people out. Hustling the sidewalks, their hands shoved in their pockets. Smoking cigarettes outside of the bars, stamping their feet to keep warm. Rory pulls his sweatshirt hood over his head. Fuck cities. He's already sick of being herded. The streetlights and the shop signs. The buttons you have to push before you walk. The busses whisking past, clunking to a stop, doors whooshing open, discharging people, moving in jerks and halts, shocks and collisions. It's electric, it grinds at your soul, it makes you want to claw at the sidewalks. Rory's whole body angles towards Nanticote as he walks.

Then he thinks of Wendy. And he sets his jaw and trudges after Pike.

An intrepid hooker in a mini-skirt and greasy long underwear stands before the glossy black storefront of a piano repair shop. Bogie's half turned to holler at her when Pike grabs him by the back of the neck and forces him on a straight line to the hotel. "Goddamn it," Bogie says. "What if that had been Dana?"

"Was it?"

"No. Fuck it. She was leech bait anyhow."

Rory looks at him. "Leech bait?"

"Leech bait. It's in Thailand or wherever the fuck. When they get a hooker that's too used up to sell to the whorehouse they tie the bitch up and dunk her a big old vat full of leech infested water. Just when she's about to nod off, they pull her out and peel the leeches off. Then they sell 'em in the market to all them poor motherfuckers they got starving over there. That's why I'm glad to be an American."

Rory just looks at him. He can't even raise his hand to slap him on the back of the head. "Please shut the fuck up," he says, and they enter the hotel.

The clerk has a face like a crushed windshield. He's sitting behind an ironwork security screen, watching TV. The lobby's clean, surprisingly clean. The maroon carpet's frayed, but there isn't a stain on it, and a four-bulb chandelier radiates a low watt light that creeps into every nook and cranny, scaring off any dirt.

"We need a room," Pike says.

The clerk leans toward them like a stack of kindling toppling. "Not here you don't," he says, jigsawed segments of skin and muscle in his face moving in conflicting directions as he speaks. He looks to have survived some terrific catastrophe and been stitched back together with baling twine.

"You've got vacancies," Pike says.

"I don't need any trouble. And you're trouble if I've ever seen it."

"No trouble at all." Pike pulls a roll of bills out of his pocket. He makes a show of them. "How much?"

The clerk hesitates, eyeing the money. Then he points at a sign spelling out the rates. "And there'll be a deposit," he says. He stares singularly at Pike, his left eye dribbling a long streak of water down his cheek. "A fifty dollar security deposit. I got doubles, I got no triples."

Pike peels bills. "We'll take a double for a week."

The clerk angles around to the room keys, never letting go of the desk. "Five-thirteen." He tosses the key on the desk.

"And send Melinda up," Bogie says, licking his lips as Pike picks the key off the desk.

CHAPTER 30

~ Smiling a sad smile that twists cruel. ~

Everything in the room's red. The carpet, the wallpaper, even the drapes on the bay window that opens down on Main Street. Red and stifling, thick with womblike air. Rory walks to the window and opens it.

Bogie looks nervous. He scratches his stomach. "Y'all mind if I watch television?"

"Go for it," Pike says, sitting on the bed and hauling off his boots.

Bogie punches the power button. The nightly news, Reagan standing at a podium. "That's the motherfucker right there," Bogie says, "that's the man."

"Reagan?" Rory asks.

"Yeah, Reagan. You got a problem with that?"

Rory shrugs. "I didn't figure you for the political type."

"I ain't political, but him right there, he's the motherfucker. He sticks up for the little guy. All over the place, too. Like them ragheads over in Afghanistan, trying to fight off the Russians. They want to be free, he's for freedom. He don't give a shit if they're a bunch of sandniggers living in caves."

"F.D.R.," Rory muses. "That's what my dad used to call him."

"F.D.R.? That don't make no sense."

"Fuckin' Dogshit Reagan."

Bogie stares at him. "I swear to God, you ever say anything like that around me again I'll kick your head in."

Rory laughs out loud.

Pike hurls one of his cowboy boots across the room, hitting the television's power button. The screen goes black.

"What the fuck?" Bogie says. "I wasn't saying nothing wrong."

"Find a way to keep yourself occupied," Pike growls. "Get a drink of water or something."

"I don't drink water," Bogie says. "Fish fuck in it."

The door to the next room bangs open, bangs shut. There's shouting in Spanish that sounds less than tender. Furniture moves, slams against the wall. Then the bedsprings pound and scream like they're being tapdanced by a rhinoceros. It seems like it goes on forever, ending finally with two loud groans. Rory starts as if from a dream, realizing that they've each been listening in perfect silence.

"They do like to fuck, don't they," Bogie says, licking his lips.

There's a knock at the door. Rory opens it to a hotel maid with flawless brown skin. She stands in the doorway, haloed by the light from the hall.

"Come on in," Pike says.

"Did you need towels?" she asks in a hollow North African accent, the door swinging shut behind her.

Pike chucks his head at Bogie, skulking in a shadowed corner of the room. "Heya, Melinda," Bogie says.

The corners of her mouth turn up coldly. Pike crumples up a bill, throws it at Bogie. "Take it in the bathroom."

They do. And a minute later, Melinda returns alone.

Pike holds out a bill to her. "You better give me another. He'll need more."

"Not for a while, he won't." She reaches into her smock and swaps the bill for a small plastic bag of heroin. "Are you the police?" She stares unblinking into Pike's eyes. She looks a mouse to his mountain, her oval brown face no bigger than one of his biceps.

"Do we look like cops?"

"You have a junky with you, but aren't junkies yourself. There are only two kinds of people that need junkies, and if you were dealers you wouldn't need me."

Pike lights a cigarette. "Doing our patriotic duty to keep the lowlifes doped. Same as yourself." He stares at the poor lady like she's an insect. Whatever they've spent the day doing, it's changing Pike. He's growing leaner, quicker. He's shedding the years like a snake sheds its skin.

Melinda doesn't look scared of him though. She looks like she's been seeing one of him all her life. "I don't mind at all making money off the likes of him." She smiles a sad smile that twists cruel. "Sooner or later I'll give him what it takes to kill him."

"You and Bogie go back a ways?" Rory asks, peeling the maroon bedspread back to the foot of the bed.

"He was a friend of my son. My son who is dead now. Do you need towels?"

Rory shakes his head.

"I'll be here all week." She opens the door. "You need more, you come to me." She closes the door.

Rory fingers two pills out of his pocket and dry-swallows them. The neighbors start up again. From dead silence to the bedsprings pounding like the mattress is on fire and they're trying to stomp it out. Then it's over, and there's just the short pop of air as Pike pulls his cigarette from his lips. "I should have found a way to get her out of it."

"You don't need to tell me anything," Rory says. It's like he's been standing in the face of a hurricane all day. Now he just wants to curl up behind something and be left alone.

Pike's voice drops a gear. "The only thing I'm telling you is that if I think Derrick's likely to be any threat to Wendy, he ain't gonna get the chance. Ever." Pike ashes on the carpet.

Wendy's face flashes in front of Rory. He smiles grimly. "I sure as shit didn't come on this trip for you."

The bathroom doorknob rattles and the door opens. Bogie's eyes are shot with red veins, his cheeks are sunken. There's still a trace of heroin around his nostrils. "What are y'all talking about?" he slurs.

Pike squashes his cigarette on the iron bed frame, lets the butt fall onto the floor. "Stay in the bathroom and keep the door closed."

"I'm fixing to go to sleep. I can't sleep in the bathtub."

Before he finishes the last syllable, Pike's at the bathroom door, slamming a palm into his chest, flattening him backwards into the tub. "If I see your face again tonight," he growls, "I just might put a bullet in it."

Rory closes his eyes. He thinks of Wendy again. It doesn't help much. He thinks of the hooker in long underwear instead, that helps even less.

CHAPTER 31

~ Like she was made combustible. ~

Cold night. Home in the cabin on the edge of the Monongahela. Their parents away, in town. She was skipping between her room and the great room, dancing to a song on the radio. Townes Van Zandt. She wore a dress their mother had made, red and white gingham. Rory sat at the dining room table, a current of cold air running down the middle of the room. Doing homework? Her breath smelled like kerosene. That's how he remembers her, but he knows it ain't right.

She had blonde hair, but not much of it. Like Rory's, when he lets it grow out, so fine it might as well be air. She had hazel eyes, flecked with the same blonde, like it'd drifted down into them. She had six teeth on the bottom, five and a half on top. They were like glass shards in her mouth. Her tiny hips pivoted side to side when she ran. She barreled over the wood floor with her belly thrust out like it was her stomach's momentum that carried her along behind it.

Their parents were in town. AA meeting? AA meeting. They were two years quit by this time, slowly losing the hatred they'd simmered up for each other over a thousand boozy nights. Of course, they both started drinking again after.

Rory was at the dining room table. Listening to the radio? Writing a letter? Cold night, the wood stove was burning. She must've opened the hatch. He wouldn't have left it open. She stuck her arm in? When the fire hit her dress, it took to it like it was made of tissue paper. Like she was made combustible. Rory jumped up, grabbed the first thing he could find, a throw blanket. Jumped on her and wrapped her in it. He could smell her cooking, just meat, he could hear her trying to scream. The screaming didn't last long, but the cooking lasted all night. Couldn't get the smell out of the house.

She knew the word for her teeth. Most of what she knew revolved around her teeth. When she was teething she'd bite holes in her hands and flick blood up and down the walls. She gnawed on everything. You'd be sitting, concentrating on something, and she'd sneak up on you, and when she sunk those teeth into you you'd jump a mile. It'd make you furious.

CHAPTER 32

~ Either you're a cop or you ain't. ~

The room's spattered with shadows that the dust-dimmed bulb hanging from the ceiling doesn't have a chance of cutting through. Derrick's on a cot against the wall, wearing a pair of jeans that look to have been used as a gearshop rag. Cotton's offered him the couch in his Airstream trailer, parked out behind the roadhouse in a grove of sugar maples, but Derrick chose the storeroom. He can't imagine himself with a bunkmate. Not at 3 AM, burning holes in his corneas staring down a cigarette, his hands twitching from lack of sleep.

Nothing to it, another night. A couple more hours, then donuts, coffee, and then out on the road. Somewhere. His exhausted brain slips with a chunk he can almost hear, like a car missing a gear. He sits up on the cot, his feet hitting the cold cement, his black hair roping down his neck. He lights a Marlboro, staring dumbly at a titty calendar on the wall. Then he pulls his .45 from under his pillow and exits the storeroom to the bar. Three quick shots of Beam in a row. Doubles. He's sweating as he lowers the last glassful. He runs his hand over his clammy stomach, the scar on his chest that runs straight down to his heart. He chases the whiskey with cigarette smoke.

It's one of those nights. He knows exactly where it's heading, the way a drunk knows the exact end of a binge before he even gets the first clumsy drink to his lips. He waits it out.

Cotton walks in a little after first light. He bites the finger of one of his leather gloves, tugging it off with his teeth. "What's up, hoss?"

Derrick's still shirtless, the Colt .45 and a half-empty bottle of Jim Beam on the table in front of him, the left side of his abdomen pulsing unnervingly in time with the pacemaker. He drags on his cigarette like to damp down the sensation. "No sleep tonight."

Cotton tosses his gloves on Derrick's table. "I don't think I've ever seen you sleep."

"Two or three hours a night. If I'm lucky."

Cotton steps behind the bar. "The heart?"

"The cure. When I'm supposed to be awake, it paces my heartbeat up. When I'm supposed to be asleep, it's supposed to pace me down. Only this motherfucker never paces down."

Cotton turns on the tap behind the bar, runs water into a coffee pot. "I didn't know it worked like that."

"The doctors tell me it doesn't." Derrick takes a last heavy drag, the cigarette filter heating between his fingers. He stamps it out in the ashtray. "But it is what it is."

The coffee maker hisses, sputters. "You ever get the urge to take it out?"

"Yep. With a dull knife and a pair of pliers."

Cotton lights a filterless cigarette with a death's head Zippo, spits a piece of loose tobacco on the floor. "There's times I worry about you, hoss."

"You'd be the first."

Cotton opens his mouth to say something else, but someone bangs on the door. Cotton closes his mouth. "Expecting company?" Derrick shakes his head, reaches for his .45. The foyer's dark. Cotton pulls a pump shotgun from under the bar, rests it in the crook of his arm, then buzzes the door open.

Jack Nolan walks in, the morning smell of highway diesel and dirty exhaust trailing with him. "Cotton," he says, nodding.

"Sheriff," Cotton returns, setting the shotgun on the bar. "What brings you out here?"

"I need a word with Derrick."

"Go ahead," Derrick says, not bothering to take his feet off the table.

Jack turns to face him. "I'm doing a favor for a friend on the Cincinnati Police Department. He gave me a message for you."

Derrick lights another cigarette.

"He did some digging. Your boy Fleischer's in cahoots with one of the black community groups working to take your shield. He gave a name. Reverend something." Jack fingers a scrap of paper out of his coat's breast pocket, tosses it on the table at Derrick's bare feet. "There's a number."

It's Klaus's number. Derrick folds it into his jeans, reminding himself to speak to Klaus about his powers of discretion. Then he looks up at the sheriff, who's still standing at the table, disgust simmering in the lines around his eyes. "You got something you want from me, sheriff?" he asks.

"I know things are different in Cincinnati," Jack says slowly. "But you're still dirty. It's all over you like a film of shit."

"How many murderers you get running around here, sheriff?" Derrick draws lazily on his cigarette. "How many child rapists?"

Jack nods slowly, like this is an argument he's had with himself before. "You're still dirty."

Derrick lets smoke filter out of his nostrils. "And you're a country dipshit who might want to stick to running down cowtippers."

Jack's already turned on his boot heel. He's halfway to the door.

"Pick a fucking side, sheriff," Derrick says after his back. "That's what it means to be a cop. You can't be more than one thing. Either you're a cop or you ain't."

CHAPTER 33

~ Still alive, curled up in the bathtub in his boxers. ~

Dreaming of Mexico again. Of border crossing. Of shedding his American skin like a snake. Then waking into the cold morning, pummeled by the stifling feeling that he has no life of his own to speak of, not here. There's laws here that Mexicans have yet to find words for. Zoning laws, decency laws, walking laws, speeding laws. Laws that proliferate like cancer cells, and behind those laws, prisons that never seem to empty, that blossom out of American small towns like tumors. Pike remembers the first breath he took the first time he crossed the Rio Grande. The air was big and clean, and it left him the same way.

He wakes and smokes a cigarette in bed, thinking. Then he checks on Bogie. Still alive. Curled up in the bathtub in his boxers, his gnarled body covered with sweat, his skin pale and twitching. He looks to have been tortured, more than once. His sparrow torso is crossed with scars, and one of his elbows is knobbed, deformed, and there's a mottled burn scar in the shape of the letter T on his left shoulder blade, splayed and crooked like the brand was put down while the kid was fighting like hell to keep it off. And he snores with the rattling whistle that comes of a nose that's been set badly. And, spreading across the kid's chest, there's a bruise. Purple-black with the force of Pike's shove.

Pike flips on the bathroom fan, lights a cigarette, staring down at it. He's had bruises like that. They ache like a fresh blow with every breath and they don't heal for a long time. They feel like they're rotting back through the breastbone, into the internal organs. He thinks hard about smothering the little shit in his sleep. He sets his cigarette on the back of the toilet and walks to his bed. He strips the blanket off and palms a pillow, returns to the bathroom. He lifts Bogie's greasy head gently and slides the pillow under it and covers him with the blanket. Then he sits down on the toilet, looking at him.

CHAPTER 34

~ He danced with one of the local girls. ~

Pike didn't make it far from Nanticonte before his money ran out. East St. Louis, an alley outside a bar, holding a tire iron. The victim got lucky, had his wallet out before Pike could get a swing off. And it was full of bills, over two hundred dollars. It was a payday that took Pike to Kansas City, where he got a job bouncing at a blues bar. Six days in, he was dealing heroin for the owner, a midget named Chuckie. She ran all the biker smack in town, funneling it from the Hell's Angels straight into the colored bars. There was an irony there that neither Chuckie nor the Angels misunderstood.

Pike was a good dealer. He was better at breaking heads. Chuckie started giving him muscle work. Pressing out the competition, clearing up debts, backing her up with the Angels. He was good at it. Then Chuckie started to notice smack missing. She hired three bikers to take it out of him, in her bar after closing. None of them left walking, and she ended up in a hospital that she never came out of, her face beat with a pair of brass-knuckles until her skin was running free with her bones.

Then Denver. He dealt the smack and bought coke to kick the smack with, planning to sell the surplus. It was a hell of a plan, but he ran out of surplus. So he got a room above a pool hall on Larimer Street, made himself available for work. All it took to know who he was you could get by looking at him, and he scored gigs using all the same talents he'd honed in Kansas City. His face was a cocaine death's head, he was on fire with knowing exactly who he was.

This was one of those nights. Dancing with one of the local girls in a honkytonk on Colfax. Dancing close. She was young, too young, all cowtown muscle and lean hunger, and she decided to pretend to mind his dancing. A cowboy stepped between them, took the girl by the arm. He was slim, his skin clear and tan. There was a thin sheen of perspiration on his upper lip, as if he knew what would come next. Pike shoved the girl away without speaking. She stumbled, recovered her feet. "Nothing's happening," she said to the cowboy. "We're just dancing."

The boy said nothing. His eyes were cavernous with pain. Pike grinned at him. The boy slipped his knife out of his pocket before Pike even saw his hand move, the thin blade slivering through the air, crossing his stomach. Those nights were bad. Pike didn't feel much on any of them. He grabbed the boy's knife hand, cranked the wrist until he heard it crunch. Then slipped his hand into his brass knuckles and hammered the boy's oval face until his legs crumbled like sandstone. Then yanked him up by his broken wrist, feeling the play in his separated bones. Pike worked on his teeth, smashing them into roughs, jerking the boy into his fist until his broken wrist had separated entirely.

Then Pike stopped. The bar was a vacuum of light and sound, sucked somewhere out into the street, the locals gaping, their dark eyes focused on him like sinkholes into their brains. The girl had collapsed into a crouch. She was sobbing slowly to herself, saying something too low for him to pick up the meaning. Pike dropped the boy's hand, let him crumple on the floor. Broken tooth fragments oozed out of his mouth, his mangled hand flopped meaninglessly at his side.

Then Pike saw they weren't looking at the boy. They were looking at him. His stomach was a plastic yellow and his intestines were poking out, glistening a light powder blue in the bar light. Pike stared stupidly and tried to poke the slippery mass back into his stomach cavity. He doesn't remember any reaction to it at all. Just the blank that was his younger self.

CHAPTER 35

~ Two of them hung up on me for mentioning
his name in the form of a question. ~

When the sun rises, he walks back into the bedroom and picks up the phone. Jack doesn't even wait for a hello. "I'm gonna need more out of you," he says. "Whatever you're doing up there, I need to know what it is."

"Or?"

"Or you get nothing from me. Or I call every officer I know in the Cincinnati Police Department and tell them you're considering doing harm to one of their own."

Pike walks the phone to the window, looks down. A huddle of three old men, blowing into their hands, stamping their feet, waiting for the bar next door to open its doors. "The other night Krieger cornered Wendy," he says. "Said he had business with her of some kind. I'm looking to figure out what kind."

There's the sound of Jack drawing off his cigarette. Then exhaling. "Krieger's partner is Christopher Vollmann," he says finally. "He's the cop who found Sarah's body. It could be Krieger recognized Wendy from her mother's murder."

Below, the bar opens and all three old men turn in unison, their faces like looking-glasses into their appetites. A wave of nostalgia for those kind of appetites washes over Pike. "Could be. You get an address for Vollmann?"

"Leave it. I've talked to every cop I know since you called me last night and the only agreement I've got out of them is you don't fuck with Krieger. Two of them hung up on me for mentioning his name in the form of a question."

Pike hangs up the phone.

Rory's out of bed and on the floor, doing pushups in his boxers, his broad back streaked with morning sunlight, breaking with muscle like a field of dense stone breaking through the soil. He turns his head to Pike. "What was that?"

Pike cleans his glasses on the bed sheet. "Krieger's partner is the cop that found my daughter's body."

Rory stops at the top of a pushup and swings to his feet. "Whoa."

Pike pulls on his boots. "You baby-sit the junky. I'm gonna talk to him."

"No way." Rory grabs his shirt off the bed. "I should be with you."

Pike looks at him. He's a brave kid, no matter his reasons for being here. "Not this time," Pike says.

CHAPTER 36

*~ He's got all the equipment of manhood
save the parts that matter. ~*

There's one Christopher Vollmann listed in the clerk's phone-book. In Westwood, a working class neighborhood on the West side of Cincinnati. Pike finds it easy, a dirty white colonial with small patch of a snow-swept dead grass for a yard, surrounded by a chain link fence. He hefts the gate open and dodges dogshit up the walk to the dirty white porch. A graying woman with the furrowed brow of a Chihuahua answers the door. "Yes?" Her hands are spattered with pottery clay, she wipes them clean on her smock.

"Mrs. Christopher Vollmann?"

She parks her hands on her hips. "I'm his mother. If you're a reporter, turn around and take a long walk towards whatever hell you believe in."

"I'm a friend of a friend."

"Right now my son doesn't have any friends."

"Who is it, please?" A woman appears in the entrance hall from one of the side doors. A young full-mouthed brunette, holding an infant in a pink sleeper.

"Don't worry yourself about it, Marie," Vollmann's mother says. "He was just leaving."

Pike moves past her. "You Christopher's wife?"

Vollmann's mother answers for her. "They're separated. This is my house. You don't step around me to get inside."

"I am his wife," Marie says. Her accent is thick French. "Do you know Christopher?"

"No. But I think my daughter did."

"I'm calling the police." Vollmann's mother turns briskly to a wall-mounted phone. " You will leave my house."

"My daughter was a hooker." Pike eyes Vollmann's mother. "I don't know how your son knew her, but I'll bet you'd rather your son's buddies weren't the ones to figure it out."

"A hooker? A prostitute?" Marie's voice trembles a little, then steadies. "He was with her?"

"That's the easiest answer."

"Shut up, Marie," Vollmann's mother says. "My son's never needed to fuck whores. At least not until you."

Marie's eyes widen like she's been smacked across the face with a wire hanger. The infant turns her face into her mother's shoulder and begins to whimper. "Excuse me," Marie says. "I must feed her now." As she exits the hallway, Pike catches a glimpse of finger-width bruises on her neck.

Vollmann's mother stares after her with a hatred that runs all the way down into her, like a bucket into a very deep well. Pike lights a cigarette and flips his lighter shut with a loud clink. Her face snaps towards him. "What do you want?"

"My daughter's dead and your son found the body. I want to know how he knew her."

"My son has never fucked whores."

"You said that. You can call the police and see how it plays out. Or you can show me where he is and I'll be on my way."

Her face twitches. "Follow me," she says, pivoting sharply on her heel. She leads Pike to a flight of stairs, up it, and down a hallway to another short flight of stairs that leads up to a trapdoor. She bangs on the trap door. "It ain't locked," a man's voice calls.

She shoves the trap door open.

Vollmann stands in front of a full-length mirror propped up against the wall. He's a crew cut blonde kid with a weightlifter's body, holding a S&W .44 in his right hand, a police issue shotgun leaning on a weight bench next to him. He rolls his head on his neck and closes his eyes, breathes, then jerks the revolver up at his own face in the mirror. He opens his eyes and takes stock of his sight alignment. Then reholsters the gun in his shoulder holster. "What do you want, Mom?"

"I have someone who wants to talk to you."

"So? What the fuck's he want?"

"Answers," Pike says.

Vollmann glances over at him. "Well. Go on ahead and say your piece, seeing how you're standing there."

"Alone."

He shrugs. "You heard him. Get out of here, Mom."

"I'm not leaving."

"I said get out of my room, Mom," Vollmann says between clenched teeth. He whips the gun out of his holster and centers the sights on his face. He flexes his gun hand, admiring the muscles as they play down his arm. "Now."

"This is my house."

"This is my room."

Pike takes his glasses off and rubs his eyes. "Mrs. Vollmann, I won't talk to him in front of you and I won't leave until I've talked to him." He replaces his glasses. "You can leave, or we can wait."

She stamps her foot in frustration, her eyes flicking between Pike and Vollmann, brimming with strange rage. Then she spins furiously and exits, slamming the trap door down behind her.

"Jesus." Vollmann twists his T-shirt on the barrel of the .44 and holds it up to the light. "She acts like I'm a fucking kid." He reholsters the gun. "What do you want?"

"You found Sarah Pike's body?"

"I did." Vollmann picks a beer can out of a stack of cans on the floor and upends it over his mouth. His Adam's apple jerks like a piston for a minute, then he wipes his mouth. "The bitch had been dead for two days and the junkies were using her as a cum dump. We had to scatter four of the filthy cocksuckers off her just to ID the body. I never smelled anything like it." He crunches the can in his fist, tosses it on the floor. "What the fuck's it to you?"

"I'm her father."

He shrugs. "Then you know everything about her there is to know. She was a junky. It ain't like any other end was likely."

Pike takes a step closer to Vollmann. "I want to know how you knew her."

"I didn't know her."

"That's the one answer I'm not gonna believe."

"Well, fuck you, then." Vollmann fumbles in the stack of cans for another beer. "Believe whatever you want."

"How'd you find her?"

"We were talking to a bum we know. He told us there was a dead girl. We investigated."

"We? You and Krieger?"

Vollmann's eyes are like pissholes in a snowbank. "Fuck you."

"Krieger's dirty," Pike presses. "Krieger's your partner. How'd you know her?"

Vollmann drops his beer and grabs at his shotgun, all in one short clean motion like he's spent hours practicing it. Doesn't matter, Pike jerks the shotgun out of his hands by the barrel, slams the butt into his nose. Vollmann yelps like a puppy, blood cascades into his cupped hands. "I think you broke it," he whines.

"It won't kill you."

"Fuck you. I'm a cop."

"You ain't a cop. You're a dumb fucking thug who wandered into a job with a pension." Pike reverses the shotgun and holds it in the crook of his arm, his finger on the trigger guard. "Hand me the .44, by the barrel."

"What the fuck are you talking about?" Vollmann looks at him, shaking his bloody head in wonderment. "I'm still a cop to the cops, no matter what they think I did. All I have to do is say your name over the telephone and I'll turn your whole world into shit."

"I'll take that chance." Pike ratchets the shotgun's slide back far enough to check the chamber, loaded. He walks to the trap door and slides the dead bolt closed. "How'd you know my daughter?" he asks, returning.

"Fuck you."

Pike flips the shotgun in his hands, slams the butt into Vollmann's temple. Vollmann lets out a thin shriek, pukes beer all over himself. Vollmann's mother tries to open the trap door. She bangs on it.

"Now that could kill you." Pike reseats the shotgun in the crook of his arm. "How did you know my daughter?"

"I didn't. I didn't." He sits down. "I didn't."

"OPEN THIS FUCKING DOOR!" Vollmann's mother screams.

Pike flips the shotgun in his hands. "One more time."

Vollmann scrabbles backwards across the floor, hitting the wall. "No. I didn't. Krieger did." He hides behind his knees. "Jesus Christ, man, I've been a cop less than a year. I'm not dirty. I did what Krieger told me to." He gulps air to keep from puking again. He's got all the equipment of manhood save the parts that matter. But remembering his half strangled wife downstairs, Pike has a hard time working up any sympathy for him. He has no doubt the kid isn't lying, he did exactly what he was told, with relish. That's why Krieger picked him as a partner.

"You ever heard of King Cambyses?" Pike asks.

Vollmann shakes his head, gulping like a drowned rat.

"He was a Persian king who learned one of his royal judges was corrupt. He skinned him alive and had a chair made of his hide. Then he made his son take his father's place, literally. He was made a judge and ordered to preside from the chair made of his father's skin. You understand what I'm telling you?"

Tears cut canals down Vollmann's blood-slicked face. "I have no fucking idea."

His mother pounds on the trap door in a desperate flurry. "I'LL COME THROUGH THIS DOOR! I'LL RIP YOUR FUCKING FACE OFF!"

"What did he tell you to do with my daughter?"

"No. Nothing. I'm telling you, we just found her body."

"Why'd you write up the report?"

"Kreiger never wrote reports if he could help it. I wrote them all." He draws up his T-shirt and dabs at the blood and snot that coat his face like an oil slick. "I never knew your daughter."

"How did Derrick know her?"

"How would I know that? He never told me nothing."

"How did he react to her body? When he saw it?"

"He was like he always was. He kind of looked at her, that's all. I don't know, I couldn't ever tell what he was thinking." He folds his hands in his lap. "Do you think I could have a beer?"

Pike nods. "COCKSUCKER!" Vollmann's mother's screeches behind him. "MOTHERFUCKER!" There's another word, too garbled to understand.

PIKE

The kid digs a fresh can of beer. "I'm sorry about your daughter."
He pops the tab. "If I'd have known she was your daughter I wouldn't
have said what I did."

"Yes you would've. And you didn't tell any lies." Pike racks the
action on the shotgun, ejecting shells until it's empty, then tosses it
on the floor. Then he opens the trap door.

Her cheekbones are bulging under the skin on her face and her
fists are clenched and red. "You get out of my house right now. Or I'll
kill you with my bare hands."

CHAPTER 37

~ I am not in the middle. ~

Pike exits the house feeling like he's been beat all over with a tire iron, and wouldn't mind beating something back. Then, just as he puts his hand on the door handle, he hears footsteps clattering towards him, too quick. He turns with a tired grin, gripping the handle of his .357.

It's Marie, without the baby. "Please, mister."

Pike's grin disappears. He takes his hand off his gun.

"Please." She stands in front of him, her breast rising and falling. "Was Christopher with your daughter? With her in a sexual way?"

"No."

Her face deflates of tension like a balloon draining of air through a pinprick hole. "Oh good." She pushes a long curl of brunette hair away from her cheek and crosses her arms over her breast, almost smiling. "Good."

"You need to leave."

She looks at him, curiously.

"Whatever's going on between those two, you need to be out of the middle."

"I am not in the middle." She flushes and her eyes dart at the house as if she expects they have ways of hearing her. "I am his wife."

"One of them is gonna kill you. Maybe both of them together."

"Oh, no, sir." She shakes her head vehemently and stamps her foot. "They will not hurt me. I am their family. My daughter, too, she is family."

Pike turns to his truck. She's the kind of woman who always ends up getting exactly what she asks for, and he doesn't have the stomach to look at her anymore.

CHAPTER 38

~ It's all the same shit to me. I don't believe none of it. ~

Over breakfast, Cotton offered Derrick a share in the Green Frog. Then proposed an expansion into other ventures. Marijuana is Kentucky's number one export, and there wouldn't be nothing to stop them from using Derrick's connections to move it. They could sell it by the bale, north into Cincinnati and beyond. None of the local law'd bother them. Growing pot on the mountains is a hell of a lot cleaner than what the mining companies do to them. It's a proposition worth thinking over, and Derrick does, spinning the steering wheel and leaning around a bend in the road, pulling a Miller Lite out of the cooler by his side.

This is how you think on things. One hand easy on the wheel, a beer in your lap, your car taking the mountain curves with quicksilver fluidity. Drinking and driving can be the most important thing in the world. It's the answer for that high lonesome feeling you can't shake any other way, it's the only way out when you've got no way out at all. It was the only thing Derrick could do for two years after getting home from Vietnam. Driving these mountains, watching the tops get sheared off them, one by one. Then driving the hell away from them.

The fuel gauge has been dipping towards E for half an hour. Derrick sees a little gas station at the peak of a long ridge. He slides the Monte Carlo into the lot, pumps his gas, and heads inside.

An old timer in a battered ball cap and a pair of bib overalls sits behind the counter, smoking a Pall Mall, reading the local paper. Derrick takes a twelve-pack of Miller Lite out of the cooler, grabs a fistful of venison jerky from the rack, drops it all on the counter. The old timer slaps the newspaper shut in disgust. "You believe this shit?"

"It's all the same shit to me. I don't believe none of it."

The old man shakes his head. "Yeah, but as young as that girl was? And them being football players, too?"

"Football players ain't immune to young pussy. It's an industry."

"But eleven years old? And two of them eighteen? And them tying her to a chair?"

Derrick feels his face harden. He softens it. "I ain't heard nothing about it."

"They had this clubhouse, back in a hollow. Like a cabin. They didn't tie her up sitting in the chair, either. They tied her up bent over it. You know what that was about. And when they were done with her they left her there two days. They say they clean forgot about her, what with football practice and all."

"Nobody noticed she was gone?"

"Her parents ain't worth a shit. Couple of damn druggies. Hell, they was probably glad to get rid of her for a day or two. She'd still be up there, I guess, but a hunter found her."

Derrick nods. "So what's happening to them?"

"Nothing but getting their names in the paper. They're saying she was into it. And that they may have got carried away, but they're real sorry about it. Hell, won't nothing happen to them, as long as they're healthy enough to play. We're going to state with these boys."

"And what does she have to say about it?"

"She don't have nothing to say. She ain't out of the hospital yet. She ain't all right in the head, neither. Not from them, she was born that way. Her parents are suing, of course. A couple of them boys come from money."

"So what do you have to say about it?"

"I say there ain't no good way I can think of to tie a retarded eleven-year-old to a chair and hump on her. But I'm an old man. I might be old fashioned."

"You might be. What do I owe you?"

The old man rings Derrick up.

Derrick hands him a bill. "They live around here? The boys?"

"Down at the bottom of the mountain." The old man counts out Derrick's change. "Anything else?"

Derrick looks out at his car through the grimy window. Then tosses a coin on the counter. "A paper. And your phone book, if you got one handy."

CHAPTER 39

~ There, I said it. ~

The Long Drop Center is the first place you look when you go hunting for bums, especially if it's wintertime and the bum's a junky. So says Bogie. The staff makes a policy of not bothering to check the bathrooms when it's cold out. Unlike most of the other charitable spots in Cincinnati, they'd rather bums get high on their toilet than turn into a icicle in some alley.

Inside, it looks like an ER waiting room on Christmas Eve, stocked with the suicidal and the deadly lonesome. The tile floor's slick with filthy slush, heaving with reeking figures. Pike's lungs contract at the shit and booze and vomit. He elbows his way to a moonfaced redhead behind the welcome desk. She sees Bogie and pulls a well-gnawed pencil out of her mouth. "I thought we found you a place."

"You did." Bogie smiles at her. "And I realized I never even stopped by to thank you." He sidles up and leans an arm on the desk. "I even bought myself a bed. A real nice one, if you ever wanna stop by. You know ladies love outlaws."

She snaps her pencil on the back of his hand. "Get off my damn desk." She glares at him and sticks the pencil back in her mouth, chewing on it like a toothless hound after a piece of jerky.

Bogie flaps the wounded hand, looking around at Pike and Rory for sympathy. He sighs and steps out of the way. "Megan, meet Pike. He's got a question for you."

Pike shakes Megan's hand. It's like a greasy lukewarm steak. "What can I do you for?" she asks him.

"I'm looking for somebody." Pike holds out the picture of Dana. "You know her?"

Her eyes trail the picture as he sticks it back in his pocket. "Are you a relative?"

Pike shakes his head. "Private investigator. Her grandmother died last week and left her some money. We want to make sure she gets it."

Megan's eyes narrow shrewdly. "I don't believe you."

"I can live with that. Where do you know her from?"

"I don't think I should tell you."

Pike leans forward a little. Her chair jerks backward, hits the wall. "No answer is not gonna be an option."

"Is there a problem?"

Pike turns his head to find a blonde in a red and white snowflake sweater, with the plump look of a woman who's yet to realize her good looks have long disappeared behind a layer of menopausal fat. "I'm Lisa Hatwell," she says in a phlegmatic voice. "If you have something to discuss, I'm the person you discuss it with." She points across the room at an office door. "Right there."

Pike follows her in and sits in front of her desk. There's a candy bowl in front of him. Bit O' Honeys, with a thin film of dust over them, like no one's yet had the nerve to take one. Lisa Hatwell doesn't sit. She stands by her chair, white knuckles resting on the desk, her lipstick lumped lips working in a rage. "You don't come in here and intimidate my staff," she says, in a voice like sandpaper on Pike's eardrums.

Pike puts the picture of Dana on her desk. "Do you know her?"

Lisa shakes a finger at him. "I fight like hell for my people. No one traipses in here and tries to intimidate them."

Pike taps the picture. "Focus."

Her eyes widen. "Am I not getting through to you?" Her voice quavers, rising. "You're in my office. You'll listen to me when I'm talking to you."

Pike lights a cigarette and eyes her like a coffee table curiosity.

"You can't smoke in here," she squawks. Her face flushes gruesomely and her red lips twitch. "Jesus Christ." She lifts the receiver of her phone. "I'm calling the police."

Pike stands and takes the phone's receiver out of her hand and places it back in its cradle. "I'll bet you scare the hell out of your staff."

His voice rumbles through the room. "Tell me where you've seen the girl, and I'll leave."

Her blonde hair helmet shudders. "Her name's Dana. She comes in two or three times a week, for feedings."

"Where do I find her when she's not feeding?"

Lisa shakes her head. "I don't know. There's a man named Rondell who she's usually with."

Pike ashes in her candy bowl. "Tell me about him."

"He's an African-American. He has a mustache and he's a Vietnam vet. His drug of choice is heroin, like her. That's all I know."

Pike turns to the door. "That's all I need."

He leaves her office, turning at the window for a last look. She stares after him, swaying a little like a thin fence post plugged into shallow dirt.

CHAPTER 40

~ I know what you are, too. ~

Bogie chews his scarred bottom lip like he's in thought, though all prior evidence should indicate otherwise. "Them Vietnam vets are weird. I don't fuck with them much. They're crazier'n hell, and they'd as soon scalp you as look at you. They've done it to one old boy, too. Took his whole scalp off."

Pike pulls a baggie of heroin out of his pocket, taps it against the dashboard. The powder dances. Bogie tries to look nonchalant. His lips tighten over his teeth, his breath hisses out like a slow gas leak. "Mount Airy Forest. That's where they hang out. Pretending they're still in country."

"You know how to find them?"

"Hell no. They're like Tecumseh up there. Even the cops don't fuck with them."

Pike flips the baggie in his fingers like he's inspecting it for quality.

Bogie's eyes roll with the motion. He licks his lips. "Fine. Fuck you. There's a bitch that used to date one of them. She hangs out over at the Dancin' Bay. Right next to our hotel, matter of fact."

Pike tosses the heroin to him and starts the truck. "Don't even think about shooting it in my truck. Last thing I need is your blood splashing around."

Bogie looks at the heroin, then pockets it. He raises his hand. "Can I ask something?"

"No," Pike says.

"I want to know if I could maybe stop by and peek at my wife and kids? Seeing as how we're right near the house."

"No."

"Goddamn, motherfucker. Please. There, I said it. Please."

"No."

"Come on. Five minutes is all I'm asking for. I won't even say nothing to them. Peek in through the window is all."

"Five minutes?"

"Five minutes. Motherfuckin' please." He looks at Rory. "C'mon, man. Help me out here. I know you got an old lady, you know what it's like."

"Sure, I got an old lady," Rory says, "She's a good old gal. Esmeralda Muckinfuch."

"There you go," Bogie says. "I knew you had a good one."

"Can't beat her when she's sober," Rory says, burrowing into the seat and closing his eyes. "Just got to when she's drunk."

"C'mon," Bogie wheedles, "help me out."

Rory waves him off.

"How's about we make a trade," Pike says. "I let you see your kids for five minutes, you shut your fucking mouth for an hour."

Bogie doesn't make it an hour. He doesn't even make thirty seconds past pulling up in front of his place, a brick townhouse in a bank of six, set back in a Corryville hill, the foundation visibly sinking. "That's mine right there," Bogie says. "See, they're outdoors, all of 'em. I ain't even got to ring the doorbell."

Two toddlers, mummified by their snowsuits, are waddling and kicking through the soot gray snow out front of the townhome. The sky above them like something vomited over the city. "They're twins," Bogie says proudly. Behind them a thin woman stands at the doorstep in a man-sized winter coat and slippers, smoking a long white cigarette. She's blonde. Her face sags on her skull. Bogie's face darkens. "And that's her. Be lucky for her if I don't cut her fucking throat and take a shit in her mouth."

"Keep a handle on it." Pike pulls the truck to a stop across the street from the townhouse. He rolls down the window and lights a cigarette.

Bogie rests his chin in his hand and stares out the window. "Goddamn, they're something." His voice breaks and tears clear trails down his filthy cheeks. "Goddamn motherfuck it. Not again."

The woman peers at the truck, sucking on her cigarette. Then she turns around and knocks on the door and says something they can't hear. The door bursts open and two enormous men sprint out of the house, waving axe handles. "They got bigger sticks since I saw them last," Bogie notes.

Pike steps coolly out of the truck, rests his right elbow on the hood, and levels his .357 at the closer of the two. "One more step and I'm putting a hole in you."

They skid to a stop, the one in front hurling his stick over the truck. "Fuck y'all!" he yells, his mouth a black hole ringed with shards of teeth.

Pike smokes with his left hand. "He's got about three and a half minutes to sit in the truck and blubber over his family. Then we're leaving. You're willing to get shot over it, that's your business."

"You don't know what that motherfucker is," the redneck says.

"I know exactly what he is. I know what you are, too. I can see it all over you, you redneck motherfucker."

The redneck puts his hands on his hips and looks down at his work boots, thinking it over. Then he nods. "We won't make no trouble."

"I figured."

CHAPTER 41

~ Use the tongs. ~

The Dancin' Bay grooves to Bruce Springsteen, the rickety metal horse over the outside entrance cantering to the vibration of the bass. Inside the air's hot with bourbon fumes and cigarette smoke, the joint hustling and bustling with locals elbowing for position. "Goddamn," Bogie shouts. "I love this motherfucking song!" He dashes through the door to the jukebox.

"Keep moving," Pike says.

Bogie turns and bellows a line from the song into Pike's face, his singing voice like a sick bull elephant. Pike takes him by the back of the neck, faces him down the bar. Bogie squirms free of Pike's grip, turns on him. "You got no heart, man, that's your problem. The Boss sings about real people. He cares about motherfuckers. Not like you."

Pike looks at him. "The only time the Boss thinks about a shitheel like you is when he's wishing all your kind had one neck. And he had his hands around it."

"Fuck you, man. You don't believe in nothing. That's your problem." Bogie pivots and heads down the bar. "Yell out if you see her," he calls over his shoulder. "She's about two hundred pounds. A big old nigger bitch."

Rory smacks him across the back of the head.

"Ow. Shit." Bogie rubs his head. "Look around you motherfucker. It's almost nothing but niggers in here. Ain't none of these motherfuckers care if I say nigger."

"I might care a little bit," says a wide black man with a patchy gray beard. He turns on his bar stool, grinning three teeth. "I might care a whole bunch."

"Shut up, Lawrence." Bogie whips out with a mock punch that snaps off an inch from Lawrence's nose. "I might kick your ass."

Lawrence slaps his knee. "Who you looking for?" he says, when he's finished laughing.

"Chandra."

Lawrence throws a thumb down the bar, towards the pool table. "Right there. She's in a good mood, too, soaking a couple of young bucks out of their paychecks."

"Told you," Bogie says to Pike. "Hold up." He sidesteps to the bar, pulls the cap off a glass jug of white and pink pickled eggs and fishes around, dirt and blood swirling off his filthy fist into the brine. He pulls two pink eggs out and stuffs one into his mouth, whole. Rory wipes his mouth with the back of his hand and feels a little faint.

"Goddamnit!" The bartender is a round white man wearing a Hawaiian shirt. "I told you about sticking your fucking hand in there, Bogie. Use the tongs."

Bogie swallows the egg without chewing. "Aw fuck you, Jimmy. I ain't dirty."

CHAPTER 42

~ They ain't nearly as well hid as they like to think they are. ~

Rory can't disagree on one point, Chandra is big. She towers over the pool table, the cue stick like a splinter in her hands. Two black kids stand behind her. The heftier of the two wearing a Griffey jersey, rolling his cue stick in his hands like he'd like to stick it in her eye socket. His skinny buddy sipping on a beer, trying not to topple under the weight of his afro. Chandra shoots, sinking the eight ball.

"A hell of a shot," Bogie says. "I mean it. One hell of a shot."

Chandra picks two fives off the side of the table. "I told you not to come around me when I'm shooting. You're bad luck, motherfucker."

"Then you'll admire my timing, see? You ain't shooting now."

Griffey's mouth twitches into a tough guy sneer. "You a cop?"

"We ain't cops," Pike answers.

Griffey's head snaps towards Pike. "Was I talking to you?"

"He's mine," Pike answers. "You talk to him, you're talking to me."

"Settle down," Chandra says to Griffey. "They ain't cops. Or at least Bogie ain't. He's most kinds of fuck up, but not that kind."

Griffey taps his cue stick on the floor, unconvinced.

"You better have a gun," Pike says to him. He unholsters his and thumbs back the hammer. "And you better be real quick going for it."

Griffey's lips twist, and for a second Rory thinks he might make a move anyway. But he tosses the cue stick on the table and stalks down the bar, his buddy wobbling unsteadily after him.

Chandra points her cue stick at Pike. "I could've soaked them niggers all night."

Pike holsters his gun and picks two twenties out of his wallet. He sets them on the pool table. "Bogie?"

"We need to know where to find them Vietnam motherfuckers that hang out in the Mount Airy Forest," Bogie says. "I heard you been up there with them."

Chandra's heavy lips purse. "What do you want with them?"

"We're looking for someone," Pike says. "One of them knows where she is."

"Well, I hope not. I went up there with a couple of them boys one night. All they talk about is scalping gooks. And camp wives. That's it, for almost four hours. Those are some motherfuckers that are lost in history." She looks from Pike to Rory. "You know what a camp wife is?"

Pike nods. Rory shakes his head.

"Gook bitches they'd kidnap out of the villages. They'd keep 'em on leashes and drag 'em around to do their dishes and suck their dicks and shit. When they wore one out they'd shoot her in the back of the head and pull another from the next village. They started talking up that shit with me too. One of them was trying to teach me Vietnamese and I was a little stoned, having fun saying the words. I mean they're funny sounding, with all them vowels. But then I caught one of them motherfuckers beating off while he was listening to me. That's when I knew it was time to get the fuck out of there."

"How'd you get away?" Rory asks.

"Oh, hell." Chandra booms a laugh. "I ain't one of those little gook bitches." She pats the front pocket of her overalls. "I carry a little .38 for just those kind of motherfuckers. I popped the hammer back and stuck it in the dude's mouth that was teaching me. I didn't take it out of his mouth until I was standing at a bus stop heading back downtown."

"So where do we find them?" Pike asks.

"That's easy. They ain't nearly as well hid as they like to think they are. There's an entrance off West Fork Road. If you got a piece of paper, I'll draw you a map."

CHAPTER 43

~ *Superior firepower.* ~

*I*t's just where Chandra put it on the map, just how she described it. A dirt lot by the side of the road. A trashcan chained to a tree and a small hidden trail winding into the snowy woods. Pike pulls a box of .357 shells out of the glove compartment and stuffs it in his jacket pocket. "Still got your gun?"

Rory pats the front of his sweatshirt.

"Don't I get nothing?" Bogie asks. "I'm a free white motherfucking man. I know how to use a gun."

"The only thing you're free of is sense," Pike says.

"Fuck you." Bogie taps his forehead. "I'm free if I say I am. This is America."

Pike thumbs open the wheel of the .357, checks the chambers. "Did you know that Parisians rioted when the police tried to hang street numbers on their houses?"

"What the fuck's a Parisian?"

"Somebody who lives in Paris. A Frenchman."

"Well why the fuck didn't you say Frenchman? Sounds like a fucking Frenchman. Ignorant motherfuckers. How in the fuck would anybody find anybody if there weren't no street numbers?"

"That's what I'm getting at. Freedom's something the French have a history of. Something dumb fuckers like you never gave a shit for at all." Pike pushing the wheel back into the frame.

Bogie crosses his arms. "You say that again and I'm leaving. I don't care how big you are, neither. I'll be done with your motherfucking ass."

Pike laughs and opens the door. He steps out of the truck and stands, eyeing the faint trail. It rises away from them through the woods up the side of Mount Airy, then disappears as the ground banks into a ravine. He sniffs the air and catches the hint of a wood fire. "Let's walk."

They swat their way through the spindly branches up the hill. Pike can't see ten feet in front of himself for the gray underbrush. He keeps his hand on his pistol, thumbing at the hammer every time one of the snow laden branches snaps or a clump of snow thuds from a tree. Then the ground starts to grade down, and the unmistakable smell of a campfire lingers in the air. Pike sidesteps down a decline to a frozen stream at the bottom and shoots a glance over his shoulder to see Rory coming, his gun tight in his gloved hand, Bogie stumbling behind, snuffling uselessly at a stream of snot. Pike hops the creek.

Something moves in his peripheral vision, a blur. He swings his .357 up, left, right. Thunk. An arrow, buried in the snow, not a foot in front of him.

"Drop the gun," a thick voice calls from the trees. "The next one goes in your neck."

Pike drops his gunhand and holds the other back at Rory and Bogie to keep still. "Who are you?"

Short breaths. Catching like somebody trying to keep a steady aim. "Drop the gun," the voice repeats. And with it, a glimpse of red, flashing off to the side of a large Scotch pine. Pike blasts a .357 slug into the tree, the report like an avalanche crack. Bark flies and a man shrieks and falls from behind it, clutching his eyes and squirming in the snow. His compound bow dropping beside him like a disseparated wing, four broadheads standing out of the arrow rest.

Pike sets the red bandanna in his gunsights. "Go get the bow, Bogie."

Bogie's face drains of blood. "What if there's more of them?"

Pike keeps his .357 steady. "Superior firepower."

"This outlaw shit's getting out of hand," Bogie mutters, creeping up the incline on all fours. He snatches the bow off the ground and scrabbles beastlike out of the man's reach. Nothing shoots at him, nothing comes after him. He stands and struts back to Pike.

"Now you're armed," Pike says. He walks to the man, who lies face-down on the ground, and crouches beside him. He grabs his neck behind the jaw, pins his face to the ground. "There more of you?"

The man tries to nod in Pike's grip.

"Where?"

"The top of the bank. Jesus, my eyes are bleeding."

Pike rolls him over. He's right. His eyes flutter open at Pike, the balls bloody red and blasted with nicks and scratches. He can't keep them open. "I'm gonna kill you," he hisses at Pike. "I'm gonna get my eyes clear and I'm gonna kill you. I'm gonna shoot you fucking dead and I'm gonna scalp you."

Pike cocks the hammer on his .357 and it clicks home, loud. "See the fix you're talking yourself into?" Pike says.

The man lets loose a phlegm-choked sob. He stops talking.

Pike pats him on the shoulder and stands. "Good boy." He waves at Bogie and Rory. "Let's go."

CHAPTER 44

~ Bogie yells, excited to have found someone
lower on the food chain than himself. ~

Two men sit on rocks in front of a firepit in a clearing at the top of the other side of the ravine. Both white and rawbone skinny, one of them wearing a Fu Manchu mustache, the other a beard, sipping delicately from bottles of Black Label beer, watching the fire. A cooler sits between them, a syringe and bloodstained belt on top of it. Behind them, a tarp shelter strung between three maples flaps miserable in the light wind. They don't bother to move as Pike and the boys enter the clearing and stand opposite the fire. If it wasn't for the frost wisping out of their nostrils, you'd think them dead.

"Gentlemen," Pike says, and waits for an answer that doesn't come.

"Fuck this." Bogie picks up a rock and tosses it into the fire. Sparks and ash shower the two men and Fu Manchu looks up languidly. His eyes are brilliantly blue over his dirty mustache and his face is oddly flat and sparse, like its been sanded off and recreated with a shortage of tissue.

"I'm looking for someone," Pike says. "One of you."

"One of us?" Fu Manchu asks in a wondering voice.

Pike nods. "A vet. His name's Rondell."

The bearded man looks up. His face is as long as the other's is flat, his nose peaking and twitching like a river rat's. "I know Rondell," he says. "What do you want with him?"

"We're looking for a girl he runs around with. Her name's Dana." Pike flashes her picture. "You know her?"

Beard deliberates, resting his elbow on his knee. "What's my stake in answering?"

"Motherfucker!" Bogie yells, excited to have found someone lower on the food chain than himself. He leaps across the fire and kicks

Beard in the hip, toppling him into the snow. Fu Manchu squeals and waves his hands in the air. Bogie whips around to face him, raising his bow and fumbling for an arrow.

Pike slams the barrel of his .357 into the side of Bogie's head. Bogie howls and drops, clutching his scalp, driving his head into the snow. Pike raises his boot to stomp his skull in, but Rory hooks him under the arm and bodily leverages him away. "Easy, big man," Rory says. Pike shakes Rory off and stares blackly down at Bogie. He's still squealing, his scalp spritzing red blood over the white snow.

Rory helps Beard to his feet. "You all right?"

"I'm okay." Beard clears his throat and retakes his seat. "Where'd that kid get that bow?"

"We took it off an old boy down by the creek," Pike answers. "He's wandering around somewhere, mostly blind."

Beard cackles, showing a set of black teeth that look like rotten stumps in sick wet soil. "He ain't even a veteran," he says. "Just Rambo crazy. We let him keep the perimeter."

Pike holsters his .357 and peels a bill out of his billfold. He tosses it on Beard's leg. "That buy an answer?"

Beard nods, secreting the bill into his boot. "Rondell's finding food. He'll be back in an hour or two. You can wait here if you want."

"Thank you," Pike says.

Beard shrugs. He fumbles a crumpled cigarette out of his jacket pocket and lights it with a match.

Bogie's calm now. Hunched on his heels, smoking a cigarette and holding his hand over the coagulating wound on his head. His eyes narrowed on Pike, like a lizard looking at a fly.

"You gonna make it?" Pike asks.

Bogie sneers. "I'm gonna make it all right. You're the motherfucker we're gonna be worrying about."

"Here." Pike lofts a baggie of heroin at Bogie. "And here." He crumples up a bill and lets it fly after the smack. "We're leaving you here."

Bogie's sneer disappears, the heroin turning him servile again. He holds the baggie up at the fire, examining it. "Y'all sure you don't need my help no more?"

"We're sure. We'll let Rondell take it from here."

"Well I'll wait here for a little while. See if you need me." Bogie reaches to the cooler for the filthy syringe.

"We'll give you a ride back to your house as soon as I talk to Rondell," Pike offers. "Your fat buddy's probably getting a little stir crazy."

"I can get back myself," Bogie says. "I'll wait here for a little while."

CHAPTER 45

~ *I've done things here that created a kind of gravity.* ~

Pike doesn't even hear Rondell approach. He just appears out of the trees, a clean-shaven black man in work boots and an army field jacket, his hooded eyes hiding behind their own darkness. He places a bag of groceries by the fire, glancing warily at Pike. "I know you, boss?" A Vietnam veteran all right. Desperate restraint around the corners of his eyes and mouth, like he's known freedom and horror in their absolute forms.

"I doubt that," Pike says.

"What're you doing here?"

"I'm here to talk to you. About a girl named Dana."

The firelight plays shadows across Rondell's dark face. "And if I was to say I didn't know her?"

"I'd say I've waded through two days of every kind of shit you can imagine to talk to her. And I'm not gonna be put off now by her pimp."

Rondell pulls a tall can of malt liquor out of the grocery bag. "I never was her pimp. I was her dealer."

"That a fact?"

"It is. And I'm retired now."

"You'd be the first."

Rondell pulls the tab on his beer can and holds it out from him, letting the beer foam drizzle into the snow. "My drug of choice was heroin." He drinks and wipes his mouth on the back of his hand. "I've been without for forty-seven days. But I can smell it." Rondell's nostrils flare and his eyes rake all over the two vets and Bogie. "I could smell it walking all the way up here. Even on the edge of the forest."

"I've got money and I want to give you some to tell me where Dana is," Pike says. "I don't give a shit if you spend it on malt liquor, heroin, or twelve-year-old boys."

Rondell looks long at Pike. "I don't know as I'd tell you anything, even if I could. I owe Dana a favor or two." His dark eyes darken, intensifying like maple sap thickening over heat. "And I don't like being called a liar."

"I didn't call you a liar." Pike taps a cigarette out of his pack and lights it, then taps out another and offers it to Rondell. "You picked a hell of a place to get clean, though."

Rondell takes the cigarette and lets Pike light it for him. "I'm a grown man and I don't like house rules." He pulls another can of beer out of the sack and offers it to Pike. "And I don't plan on being here forever."

Pike takes the beer and cracks it. "Where are you going?"

"Out west. I've got a cousin in Colorado." Rondell breathes in steadily and looks around at the woods as if he's already gone. "Anywhere but here. I can't take it here anymore. I've lived out west and you can still be left alone out there. At least some. It's disappearing fast, but at least every little motherfucker in the world isn't breathing down your neck every minute of every day." He burps silently into his hand. "We're too close around here."

"You talk like an ex-con."

Rondell nods. "I've found all kinds of ways to get institutionalized." A shadow crosses his face that isn't from the firelight.

"I made it west for a while," Pike says. "To feel what you're talking about. I made it further, too, into Mexico. You really can be left alone there. All the time and without having to beg for it." Pike drinks, and the malt liquor slicks down his throat, leaving an oily aftertaste. "Or at least you could. I don't know how it is now. We spread fast."

"Like cancer." Rondell stares into the fire. "What in the hell did you come back for?"

Pike hesitates. It's a question he asks himself no more than four or five hundred times a day. "I've done things here that created a kind of gravity," he says slowly. " Having the right to move away would be like having the right to claim not to have done them in the first place." He's conscious of Rory watching him carefully, taking in every word.

"Take it from an ex-con, the market in redemption is running low." Rondell chuckles with the resonate boom of a thunderhead. "Hell, there's history everywhere. Get out as quick as you can. That's my advice."

Pike's smile garrotes his face. "You're probably right." He wants to say more. There's something about Rondell that tugs at him to keep talking. But he forces it down. "I need to find Dana."

Rondell nods. "So you said. But I need to know why before I tell you where."

"I need to talk to her about my daughter."

"Your daughter." Rondell's eyes hold steady on Pike. "Is your daughter in some kind of trouble?"

"No trouble at all. She's dead."

"Ah." Rondell takes a last swig out of his can of malt liquor and empties the backwash out in the snow. "What was her name? I used to know some of Dana's friends."

Pike nods, having already thought of that. "You might have been my daughter's dealer, too. If you were I'm gonna have to ask you other questions."

"If I was, I owe you other answers."

"Her name was Sarah. She had blue eyes."

Rondell sits with his empty beer can in his hand, groping through the underbrush of his memory. Then shakes his head. "No. I didn't know her."

"Good," Pike says, and he means it. "Back to Dana, then. Do you know where she is?"

"You need to talk to her mother."

"I have. She's done with her."

"She's never done with her. She knows where she is. She wouldn't piss on her if she was on fire, but she knows where she is." Rondell watches Pike deliberately. "She gets off on watching her fuck up her life. It's the only thing she gets off on. It's the same feeling we used to get watching the country girls in Vietnam turn to hooking in Saigon. After we'd napalmed their villages."

CHAPTER 46

~ Did we do something to you, mister? ~

A plantation farmhouse sitting a ways off the highway, the driveway paved and winding through the forest into the hollow, past a snowy field and stables. There's a detached garage, the door lifted open a few feet. Light and heat spill out onto the blacktop, a stereo inside blares Springsteen.

Derrick pulls to the side of the driveway fifty yards back from the house and jogs to the garage. He hunches down, checks under the door. Two flat-topped boys with the hood lifted on a Chevy, staring down into the engine like engaged in a kind of haruspicy.

Derrick boots the garage door down behind him. It hits home with a heavy chunk. Both boys look up in unison, Derrick meets the first with his brass knuckles, tearing his nose into a cartilage smear across his cheek, all but swiping it off his face. The boy crumbles in a wash of blood, Derrick pulls his .45 with his free hand, plants the muzzle on the second boy's forehead. "Kick him."

The boy stands still.

"I said kick him." Derrick thumbs the hammer back. "Kick him, honey."

The boy kicks his friend in the ribs, but he doesn't seem to notice. Too busy fumbling at the mangled thing that used to be his face.

"Now unbuckle his belt and pull down his pants."

"Did we do something to you, mister?" the boy quavers.

"Nothing I can think of. But if you don't do what I tell you, I'll put holes in your head."

The boy doesn't move. "I'm scared."

"Sure you are. But as of right now you both get out of this alive. It doesn't have to be that way."

The boy finds his friend's belt buckle. He unbuckles it, pulls his jeans down to his knees. His friend whimpers, blows bubbles in the pool of blood haloing his head. His legs are white. His underwear is streaked with shit.

Derrick steps back. Takes a seat on a toolbox and picks up a monkey wrench. He holds it up against the light, then hands it to the boy. "You can use this." He lights a Marlboro, ready to watch. Already making plans to keep what is his.

"I don't want to," the boy says, his chin trembling.

"This ain't about desire," Derrick says. "It's about power. Ain't anybody taught you anything, you dumb cracker?"

CHAPTER 47

~ I wasn't exactly devoted. ~

She opens the door on the first knock, holding a large gin fizz that barely fizzes, her breath a wash of alcohol that makes Pike's eyes water. "Mr. Pike," she slurs.

Pike pushes past her into the living room, takes a calm appraisal. Poodles and more poodles in gold gilt frames. "What did you say your husband's name was?"

"I didn't." She waves her glass angrily, sloshing gin on the carpet. "You will leave now, Mr. Pike."

"You will tell me where Dana is, Mrs. Jennings, or you will be seriously fucked."

"I told you, Mr. Pike. My daughter's a junky whore. I don't keep track of junky whores."

"Sure." Pike slivers a cigarette between his thin lips and bends to touch it to his Zippo's flame. "Where's your husband?"

She flinches as if he'd raised his fist to hit her. "Leave. Now. I don't care what you've heard. It doesn't give you the right to come into my house and level accusations at me."

"I can understand you not having any pictures of your daughter," Pike continues. "But where's the rest of the family photos? You and your husband never took a picture together? Never went on vacation?"

Her lips are a gray line carved out of a chunk of lifeless clay that just happens to look like her face. "My husband was a pathetic man. He cut his own throat with a steak knife."

"Couldn't have been too pathetic," Pike saya. "A steak knife would mean you'd have to saw." He looks her over. "What you said last time about your daughter never being molested. That ain't entirely true, is it?"

She sits down, her face changing and rearranging, as if her hatred is an iron cast that Pike's managed to crumble, and she's working to rebuild it as quickly as she can. "Frank never touched her. Never. That was put into her head by a graduate school therapist."

"What was she in therapy for?"

"She was having trouble sleeping. By the time we understood what was happening, the therapist had convinced her that it came from a fear of sexual attack by her father. He invented a history, and when we disproved the events he constructed, he altered the details to fit new events."

"And you didn't believe her?"

"I don't believe her, Mr. Pike. My husband was a devoted father. He was other things, too, of course, many of which I know nothing of. But the one thing I know for certain he wasn't is a child molester."

"Then why'd he gouge his windpipe out with a serrated knife?"

Mrs. Jennings looks at Pike. "You had a daughter, Mr. Pike. Devoted fathers are always in love with their daughters. They sneak kisses on them. Sometimes they even get a visceral thrill out of their wriggling bodies. They always wonder where the line is, and they're always fearful they might have crossed it. We've taught them to be." She sips her gin, restoring a hint of color to her face, but only a hint. "You should know all of this, Mr. Pike, I'm sure Sarah was a lovely young lady." There's a small note of triumph in her voice that makes Pike think of doing things to her that he hasn't thought of doing to a woman in a long time.

"I wasn't exactly devoted."

"Ah." The small note of triumph is no longer small. "Perhaps that's for the best."

Pike sticks his thumb and forefinger under his glasses and rubs his eyes. "I need to talk to Dana."

"And if I told you I had no idea where she was? That I don't track whores."

"I'd know better." His grin would look better on a corpse. "And I have all the time in the world."

CHAPTER 48

~ Pike leads her eyes to the truck with the barrel of his gun. ~

The Third Street bridge covers a half block on either side of the street, sheltering a long swath of oily concrete that's been turned into a shantytown. Hacked pieces of corrugated tin and sheet insulation form lean-tos on the iron girders, and tents pitched out of greasy tarps and broomsticks run right up to the snow drifts. Shambling forms huddle around fire pits pounded out of the cement, smoking, drinking, spitting into the fires.

"This is it." Pike's face is steady, but his hands are twitching.

"We could stop here," Rory says. "There's some things maybe it's better not to know."

A thin wisp of snow curls down the snow bank edging the shanty-town. "We crossed that line a long time ago," Pike says.

"Not yet," Rory says. "Whatever it is we're doing, we've long stopped doing it for Wendy. We can turn the truck around. Hell, we can be back at The Oxbow inside of four hours, eating breakfast. Walking's better than running away."

"To be the men who want the ocean without the awful roar of its many waters?" Pike rests his hand on Rory's shoulder and squeezes it firmly. Then opens the truck door. "Besides, crawling ain't no good at all."

Rory shakes his head, following him. "Do you ever have any quotes that fit the fucking occasion?"

There's no time for Pike to answer. A black junky leaning lazily on a beam a few feet back from a trashcan fire, a blood spattered syringe hanging from his left hand like it's a cigarette. His eyes sliver at their approach. "You want something?"

"Dana."

"White bitch?"

Pike nods. "Where?"

The junkie chuckles cannily, his eyes flicking at a tin roofed shanty about twenty feet away. "Under that nigger over there."

Pike's there, something dark singing in his veins. He rips the hunk of tin away from the beam and sends it reeling like a drunken dancer across the dirt, and strips the blanket off them. His broad black back, her bruised pink arms strapped across it. Pike boot nails him in his ribs, lifts him spinning in the air. He lands with a grunt on his back in the coal dust and rust, his wet dick wagging ruthlessly in the black air. Dana breathes in sadly, her blue-nailed fingers still clutching at the spot where his back had been. Her pink cunt still open and round, like a misshapen little mouth.

"Get up," Pike growls.

She feels around for her clothes. The man's switchblade opens with a sharp snick. Pike turns. He's inches away, still naked from the waist down, his dick swaying like a noose and his thin knife slicking through the air for Pike's jugular. Rory shoulder-rams him, spoiling the knife blow. He stumbles, turns to face the kid. Rory catches him on the point of the jaw with a sharp uppercut, reeling him back, then slips a knife jab and shoots a one two combination into his nose, popping it like a tomato.

He should drop. But he doesn't. Blood swarms from his nose, cascades down his shirt. His eyes burst with rage and his big body tenses to explode at Rory. Rory dodges a wild roundhouse right, but he doesn't see the knife that follows, cutting through the air in a jagged arc.

Pike's gun flames, booms. The .357 slug pounds his black chest like a sledgehammer, sucking flesh, blood and air into a pink vaporous hole that explodes out his back. He takes a stagger step at Rory, his knife still raised. Pike fires again, at his knee this time. He drops, his bloody shin and crooked foot slinging off his leg, attached only by a thread of skin. He tries to scream, tries to howl, but he doesn't make a sound. The hole in his chest froths and bubbles. And he dies.

Rory turns his head, pukes.

PIKE

Pike points his gun at Dana. Her hand covers her mouth and the irises of her eyes dilate on the barrel. Pike leads her eyes to the truck with the barrel of his gun. "Get the fuck in."

CHAPTER 49

~ I ain't feeling bad about killing him. ~

Rory stands in the bathroom doorway, watching Pike jerk Dana's arms around the toilet and fasten her wrists together with a zip-tie. Pike's face is an animal blank. Rory's scared to leave her alone with him. "I'm gonna kill you," Dana hisses at Pike. Her heroin high is wearing off and she's becoming less amicable by the minute. Pike pulls the zip-tie tight with a sharp jerk, then turns from her and steps around Rory into the hotel room. Rory shuts the bathroom door.

Pike draws his cigarettes and lighter out of his pocket and places them on the nightstand. He pulls a cigarette out of the pack, lights it, and sits down on the bed. Then his hands begin to tremble. First the left, then the right. He drops the cigarette on the floor and his arms lower to the bed like girders and he clenches the bedclothes in his fists. The trembling spreads up his arms and through his chest. His jaw clamps down. His neck steels. His arms bulge and jerk. The whole bed shakes, banging and rattling on its frame, like there's something caged in his chest, ramming its body against his ribs, like he has to use every muscle in his body to keep it from pawing its way out.

Then, as quickly as it came, the trembling drops away and his chest falls. Pike grabs the trashcan beside the bed and snatches it up to his face and pukes.

Rory picks his cigarette up out of the carpet. He puffs it twice to keep it alight and waits for Pike to stop puking. When he does, Rory takes the trashcan out of his hands and gives him the cigarette. Pike draws off it.

"There was nothing else you could have done," Rory says. "I'd have done the same if the roles were switched."

"I ain't feeling bad about killing him."

"Then what?"

Pike's face warps into an ugly smile. "Let's get what we need out of her. I've had enough of junkies to last me a lifetime."

CHAPTER 50

~ You always have a choice. ~

Dana's crying when Pike enters the bathroom, her shoulders trembling softly against the backdrop of the toilet seat. When he shuts the door behind him, her back stiffens like glass setting. He cuts the zip-tie free from her hands, takes her by her arm, lifts her up and sits her on the toilet. Then he hands her a lit cigarette. She sucks on it greedily, finishes it in under a minute. When she's done, her face is crunched back into place. Tough and cold and ugly enough to make Pike want to look away. "I should have known I'd see you again," she says.

"I'm hard to shake."

A grin hardens on her face like a kind of rigor mortis. "I've heard all about it."

Pike pulls his glasses off and cleans them on his T-shirt. He resets them on his nose. "There's a man who started hanging around my town, asking about Wendy. I need to know who he is."

"You need my help. That's delicious." She crosses her legs, the filthy slick of her jeans mirroring the bathroom light. "What's his name?"

"Derrick. A white trash cop. About my height." He stops talking. She's begun to chuckle to herself.

"Derrick was Sarah's pimp," she says, giving the word a delectable pop. "You could have figured that out."

"I had the idea, but I need more." Pike takes in her face like he's back in Juárez counting cards. He wants every glimmer of thought that runs over her brow, he wants to see through her skull to her firing synapses. "Would he have killed her?"

She isn't difficult to read. She gapes at him, stupefied. "You're hard-headed, I'll give you that," she says in a kind of awestruck tone. "She overdosed. On heroin. She was a junky. She'd been trying to overdose since I met her. She got lucky is all."

Pike nods. "When you brought Wendy to me, you looked scared. Like you were running from someone. Was it him?"

It's only after a minute or two that she manages to close her mouth. "I was scared of you, you dumbshit. I'd heard all about you."

Pike gathers the fist of his right hand in his left and doesn't talk for a long time. "Do you know what kind of pimp Derrick was?"

Dana shakes her head, something like pity on her face. "No, I guess not. I never did work for him."

"Know anybody that did?"

"There's a girl named Annabelle, I think. Or at least there used to be."

"Do you know where she lives?"

She nods.

"Will you show me?"

"Do I have a choice?"

CHAPTER 51

~ The sun sheds her and she shrinks in her chair. ~

Dana totters away from them, winding down the sidewalk through Clifton's gaslight district, shaking her head to herself like she's seen a circus animal perform some trick she didn't think possible. Rory sticks his hands in his sweatshirt pockets and looks at Annabelle's house. It's a long yellow-sided shotgun shack, hunched among the Queen Anne and Renaissance Revival mansions. Hooking for Derrick must not have been too bad. "Ready?" Rory says to Pike.

Pike doesn't say anything in return. He looks like he's been running through the woods all night, and just came across a landmark that reminds him he's still miles from home. He moves slowly to the front door and knocks.

"Yes?" a woman's voice peels out.

"Annabelle?"

The door opens. She's blonde and built slight, almost like Wendy. She's no girl, though, that shows in her wide blue eyes. "I'm Annabelle."

"You used to work for Derrick Krieger?"

Annabelle's face breaks in a strange smile. "You're cops, right?"

Pike nods. "Something like that."

Annabelle holds the door open. "Please, come inside." She waves them into the living room. "Sit down. I can't say I'm exactly happy. But I've been waiting for this."

Rory sits beside Pike on a leather Manhattan couch. The walls are lined with books and there's a thick paperback volume with a horse on the front open on the mahogany coffee table. She takes a matching armchair across from the couch and sits crosslegged. The clear winter sun lights on her from the skylight above and Rory's chest caves a little. She's the kind of whore he thought only existed in movies.

"We're not cops," Pike says.

Annabelle cocks her elfin head curiously. In the sunlight, her face changes every time she moves, breaking into some new gradient of itself, each more compelling than the last.

"My daughter worked for Derrick," Pike continues. "Sarah was her name, but she's dead."

"I knew Sarah. She looked like you, a little." Annabelle slides a small plate with a pack of rolling papers and a bag of Drum tobacco from under the book on the coffee table. "What do you need from me?"

"Anything you can tell me," Pike says, but his face calls him a liar.

Annabelle plucks a rolling paper out of the pack. "Derrick is a cop who has an unseemly interest in whores." She expertly fingers a groove in the paper. "There's not a whore in this city who doesn't know what he is. Nor a cop. Nor anyone else. There might be a few in the suburbs who haven't heard, but not here in the city." She taps a mound of tobacco into the rolling paper. "He's a killer, too, of course. But everybody knows that, too."

"Who?"

"That boy he shot in the back. The one that started the riots." She rolls the paper between her thumbs and forefingers. "He wasn't a suspect in anything, and he wasn't trying to get away. He was one of Derrick's dealers who'd made the mistake of pinching heroin to sell for himself." She rolls the cigarette. "None of that is anything you needed me to find out, though."

A cloud passes over the sun and Rory watches Pike's face blot out in the sudden gloom. There's something obscene in the dogged way he's going after this. He's disintegrating, and in the face of this woman he doesn't have a chance. Rory has a sudden urge to throw an arm around his shoulders and raise a hand, to signal to the referee that this fight's over. "I need to know what he was like. When he was with you, what kind of pimp was he?"

"He wasn't my pimp," Annabelle answers. "He never took money. He was more of a, well, interested party."

The sun returns and flows in from the picture window behind Pike. It backlights his massive form and shades his face, illuminating

Annabelle in a brilliant yellow wash. "I need to know if he could have killed Sarah," Pike says in a low voice.

Annabelle lights her cigarette. "He could have." A stream of blue smoke flows from her nostrils and floats away in the sunlight. "But he didn't. I was at his place the night she died. All night."

The words quiver in Pike's face like they've been delivered with an electric prod. He rubs his knees and slowly stands, holding his right hand out to her. "Thank you."

The front door opens and slams shut. A girl of maybe seven steps inside and stamps snow off her oversized snow boots. "I'M HOME!" she calls.

"We're right here," Annabelle says. "There's no need to shout."

Rory's backbone's jolting like he's been hit by lightning. The little girl nods her blackhaired head at him and she clomps across the living room, disappearing down the hallway on the other side of it. Rory can't speak. He's only vaguely conscious of Pike next him.

When he finally speaks, Pike's voice is thick and weird. "Who is she?"

"She's my daughter." Annabelle's eyes flick from Pike to Rory.

Pike's right hand moves to his shirt pocket for his cigarettes, like of its own accord. "Who's her father?"

Annabelle's cigarette droops in her hand and the sun sheds her, seeming to shrink her in her chair.

Pike lights his cigarette, his chest swelling with smoke. "Derrick," he answers for her.

Annabelle nods. "Like I said, he didn't take money. In fact he even paid us a sort of child support. The only condition was that they never see him. Those were his terms and ours."

CHAPTER 52

~ He knows he ain't going anywhere. ~

The highway cuts through the snow-covered foothills like a wet black wound. Rory's nauseous just thinking about the curves to come. He swallows a handful of pills that make a sick crackling sound as they clear his dry throat. "What do we do now?"

Pike takes a curve too fast, easing his hands on the wheel, letting the tires slip on the wet blacktop, then find their own way back to traction. "Nothing."

"We don't tell nobody? About him dealing drugs and shooting up black kids?"

Another curve. Pike grips and slams the wheel around it like the truck's a part of himself he's trying to beat into shape.

"That's something you tell somebody about. You sure as hell don't sit on it and wait for him to kill somebody else."

"Who are you planning to tell?"

"Somebody. The newspapers."

"When we get back give a call to the *Enquirer*. I'm guessing they ain't gonna move real quick on a story that could restart the riots. On your say-so alone."

"Then I'll try the black papers. I know there's got to be at least one black paper."

"There's plenty of them. And you ain't gonna win any Pulitzers telling blacks in Cincinnati the cops are corrupt. It'll dissipate into the air like every other story that comes out of the black papers."

"What happened to all that shit you were saying about oceans without water or what the fuck ever?"

"The particular shit covering this state won't be purged by us. I guarantee you of it."

"You don't think he killed her anymore, do you?"

Pike shakes his head. "If anybody killed her, it wasn't him."

"Well." Rory nestles back in the seat. He closes his eyes. "Shit," he says. He goes to sleep.

Pike cracks his window, lets a cool slip of air run in over his face. He watches the hills run past and forces his mind to empty, to concentrate on the road ahead of him. He could clear out. Back to Texas, or maybe Colorado. There couldn't be anyone left alive he knew. The way the people he ran with lived, they had to be dead by now. But just in case, he could try the Black Hills or head up to Montana. His days out west had never carried him that far north. Or he could make it through Texas and cross the border, like he'd done a thousand times before. Mexico is freedom. Mexico is washing yourself of all the shit that comes from making it in the North. Mexico is shaking Sarah, Alice and Derrick in one clean move. And this time he'd be crossing clean. Nothing illegal.

It sounds good. It sounds like the best idea he's ever had. He gets tight in his chest as if he's already on the road, already driving all night. Sucking down a Styrofoam cup of coffee, watching the snow melt off and the land empty. Clean highway air, with a hint of his exhaust on it, drifting to him through his cracked window.

Then his eyes water. He thinks of Sarah's corpse lying alone in the abandoned house. Of the junkies scuttling over her and mauling her and ejaculating into her. His backbone jolts and his eyes twitch. He thumbs his glasses up his nose and he knows he ain't going anywhere.

CHAPTER 53

~ Dragging their beer cart in a Sisyphean arc. ~

A tin-roofed roadhouse across from a gasket factory in Cincinnati, the building facing sideways into an abandoned lot, like a piece of debris that's blown out of the factory's orbit and spun to rest at a cockeyed angle. Inside it's a dim-lit tunnel with a high Formica bar and a pockmarked Hispanic bartender, leaning on the bar and watching news on the television, a toothpick hanging from his thin lips. The only patron is a gray-bearded man in a dirty Reds ballcap.

Derrick sits down on a stool. The bartender looks at him out of the corner of his eye, rolls the toothpick in his mouth and looks back at the television. "Beam," Derrick says, "and a Miller Lite." The bartender fetches the drinks, his eyes never leaving the television. There's a lit-up Budweiser display over the bar, quarter horses pulling a beer wagon. The horse's feet move when you look at it right, dragging the beer cart in a Sisyphean arc. Derrick drinks the beer and drinks the shot, thinking about his life as little as possible.

Commercial break. The bartender divines Derrick's ready for another and opens a can for him. Derrick nods by way of thanks.

"You just start?" the bartender says.

"Start?"

He jerks his head in the direction of factory. "I ain't never seen you in here before."

"I was driving by and needed a drink," Derrick says. "You was the only place around."

The bartender wipes the leathery counter down and tosses his rag under the bar. "Most of our customers are over at the factory." The commercials run off, and his attention wanders back to the television.

"I retired," the old man says, out of nowhere.

Derrick looks at him, but the old man doesn't return his gaze, he's staring at the television.

"Good place to retire from," Derrick says.

"Yep," the old guy says. "Good benefits." He doesn't say anything else. He lifts the little beer glass to his mouth in quiet twenty-second intervals, he fills it every eight drinks. His elbow and hands work like they're running on an engine, and the bartender never lets him go dry. It's a machine that can run forever without stalling. Retired, hell.

The bartender pulls about thirty shot glasses and sets them up on the counter, starts to filling them with bourbon. "They've got a fifteen-minute break coming up," he explains to Derrick. He finishes with the bourbon shots, starts to popping beer tabs on Budweiser cans. "They're gonna want them set up."

Derrick stands, drops a five on the counter. He leaves the bar without looking back at the old man, still lifting his glass of beer in twenty-second intervals like he's on a spring. Derrick cracks his knuckles as he steps out of the bar.

BOOK III

You are the moderate man, the invaluable understrapper of the wicked man. You, the moderate man, may be used for wrong, but are useless for right.

— *Herman Melville*

CHAPTER 54

~ Pike is sad for the dumb thing. ~

Pike can't take the stand for more than an hour. He's never been able to. He never was much of a hunter, even as a kid. He had no quiet. His mind was a riot and he missed as often as he hit, guts-hooting more than one buck. Luckily, his father had quiet in spades, and no hard words for him ever. He'd simply take the lead, tracking the gutshot buck with the boy and showing him the signs, and then when they found it, which they always did, shooting it cleanly to put it out of its misery. He moved with that same quiet deliberation in everything he did, and he never missed, not when it was food on the table.

The hunts brought them together. As did the butchering, in the cold tent made of sheet plastic in the back yard, listening to country and western music and laughing at each other over the meat. That they were poaching Pike didn't learn until later. There was land and it was open and they needed the food. If anything, Pike considered the land as theirs. They'd taken deer in every hollow and on every hill and he figured they'd marked it out with every buck they'd brought down. Land wasn't something you could own by virtue of a piece of paper.

Now the deer are all but hunted out. You're lucky to see one in an entire season. But Pike doesn't hunt for food anymore. He just gets a need to walk in the woods, carrying his father's lever-action Winchester 30-30, remembering the old steadiness he got from watching the old man work. It brings him back to the man he wanted to be when he was a boy. It makes him forget what he blundered into being later.

Pike left his father's home hard. He knew the way the people in town looked at the old man, and he didn't want it to be anything they could hang on him. There was a girl Pike had brought home and she had a mouth on her. The old man tried to get between them. Pike threw him through the front window. Then found him outside and punched him in the jaw until his jawbone cracked like an old piece of dry wood, the girl hanging from his back, spitting and screaming for him to stop. That was the last time Pike and the old man spoke.

In a long life of regrets that may be the greatest. But, then, when you get to a certain measure, there's no point in weighing one against the others. It's enough that when Pike hunts he can still feel the old man with him. Steady and quiet. His impossible measure of deliberation and kindness shown in the smallest of his movements.

Pike catches a spot of brown at the tree line of a small glade and crosses the meadow to it. He stops and focuses. Can't be. But it is. A buck, sunk into the snow, not moving. Pike steps closer. The buck's ribs and spine show and the thing's eyes are hollowed into his head. He's dead. Pike hunkers down about ten feet from him and rests the rifle across his knees. He's the first buck of his size that Pike's seen in decades. Twelve points and not less than 250 pounds. Pike takes in a reverential breath and lets it out slowly.

The quiet in the old man is what Pike needs now. To pass it on to Rory. The kid's burning up from the inside and anyone can see it. He comes from a people that had no quiet whatsoever. They were all over the place, running on hostility like an engine runs on gasoline, rolling around their house and taking each other out in series of small hatreds and collisions. The kid does what he can to damp down the noise they've filled him with, their burnings and their suicides, but they ain't made that drug yet.

But that's only half the story. Pike runs his right hand over the riflestock, the wood worn glasslike by his father's hands and his. What's ripping around in the back of Rory's head right now ain't got anything to do with his family life. Pike finds a cigarette in the breast pocket of his coat and looks into the shrunken eyes of the buck and lights it.

The buck's nostrils flare at the smoke. His head rises up, huge and antlered and terrible, and he paws at the ground for footing. Pike stands and lets the cigarette fall out of his mouth and brings the rifle to his shoulder. The animal's eyes are suddenly alive, round and black as they cling to Pike's. He snorts a barrage of frost and turns to limp away, but stumbles almost to his knees.

Then Pike sees the blood in the snow and the hole in his side that leaks black blood. Some stupid asshole has shot him and let him wander away to suffer. He was playing possum.

Pike's sad for the dumb thing. He puts a bullet in it.

CHAPTER 55

~ The beating has taken his bowel control. ~

Evidently Christmas means something to Dick Fleischer. His Blue Ash Tudor home is choked with colored lights and icicle trim and he has a full-sized Santa on his lawn, stepping into a chimney that throbs red and releases timed chugs of smoke. Not to mention a set of reindeer strapped to a sleigh that's bigger than Derrick's Monte Carlo, and more minor pieces and nativity scenes then Derrick has the time or inclination to count.

Christmas isn't much of anything to Derrick. All he has is a five gallon can of gasoline and a pair of brass knuckles. He looks up and down the street. Nothing moving. He lifts the gasoline can and pours the contents over Santa and tosses the can to the side. Then sparks a match and watches the plastic monstrosity whoosh into the winter sky, a pillar of fire. He starts a cigarette and leans back against his Monte Carlo to wait. His heart's pounding steady, he feels relaxed and even.

Derrick's not a particularly good fist fighter. He's never boxed and he doesn't take a punch any better than any other cop who's better used to giving beatings than receiving them. But his heart gives him the edge. He can always count on the other guy's to beat too fast, to fill his head with wobbly giddiness, to spark his nerves with twitchy adrenaline. Derrick's stays as cool and even as an engine.

It doesn't take long. The lights in the house flick on and Fleischer bursts out the front door. An aluminum baseball bat cocked back over his shoulder. His satin pajamas ballooning in the winter wind. Panic, in the way he's sweating.

Derrick waits for him to get within five feet and flicks his cigarette at his eyes. Fleischer ticks his head to the side, it flashes by his cheek. He should have taken it. Derrick's in close. Fleischer jerks the bat in an awkward loop and Derrick blocks the downswing with his forearm, hooking a right into the side of Fleischer's head, landing the brass with a solid thud.

Fleischer pulls the bat back for another swing. Derrick pounds him again, this time on the side of the head. There's a sick crunch and Derrick hits him one, two, three more times in the same spot. Fleischer's ears bubble blood and he sags, slipping sideways onto the lawn, all his rage and forward momentum disintegrating.

Derrick doesn't let him fall easy. He's good with the knuckles. He lands three more rights into the side of Fleischer's mouth before he makes it to the ground. Fleischer's molars crumble like candy corn and he collapses in the snow, his mouth open and running with blood and teeth.

Derrick crouches in front of the fat man's face. "The thing is, I doubt you could stop what you started even if you wanted to," he says. "I'll probably lose my badge and I'll probably get sent up on charges and there probably ain't a damn thing you can do about it."

Fleischer makes a gurgling sound in his throat, as if he's trying to speak and vomit at the same time. Blood and puke trickles out of his mouth.

"I'VE CALLED THE POLICE!" a fat blonde woman yells from the door. She's standing with two fat children at her sides, holding her hands over their eyes. They're all three wailing, their bodies jiggling like pudding.

"This is just the beginning. When they pull my badge, I'll take you somewhere I can spend some real time with you." Derrick pulls the brass knuckles off his hand, examines his fingers. Already shadowing with purple bruises. Derrick slides the brass knuckles in his back pocket. "The best part? You were right. The nigger kid was my dealer. I sponsored him because he ran a clean business, for the kind of business it was. He didn't start wars that got kids shot up and he didn't work on getting new customers hooked. He provided a service that was more decent than most. If he hadn't been a pedophile he'd have been the perfect nigger."

Fleischer's eyes glisten with hate and pain. A new stink rises off him. The beating has taken his bowel control.

The woman starts to scream something else, but her voice is cut off by a sob.

"I want you to think about all the dealers I know," Derrick continues. "I want you to lay here until the ambulance comes, guessing how much heroin I have my hands around. Then, on the way to the hospital, while you're trying to spit my name out through your broken jaw, I want you to calculate up how many junkies there are in this city who'd rape your wife, even as fucking ugly as she is, for a five-dollar fix."

CHAPTER 56

~ It's a slight miserable thing of a nod, like a half-dead swallow trying to find its wings. ~

The winter moon hangs low and cold, flickering streaks of moonlight over the black forest. Rory's dark cabin fits snugly into the snow, a wisp of wood smoke trailing out of the stainless steel chimney. It's late and the fire in the pot-bellied stove has long since burned down to embers. Rory's awake in his bed, his smooth-worn quilt lying on his bare legs like the touch of a young girl. He's been waking by degrees for awhile now.

The doorknob rattles, gently. Rory's breath catches in his throat. He's suddenly all the way awake. Something moves around the house and the window clatters. Then a hand thrusts through it and taps up the latch and the window creaks open. Rory lays motionless, his right hand snaking out from the covers, reaching under the bed. Small logs clamber down the woodpile and a figure sticks a foot through the window, finds the table. Then hops noiselessly down and reaches back to latch the window.

Rory sits upright, lifting a sawed-off sledgehammer handle. "Stand right where you are."

"It's just me," she says.

"Wendy?"

She nods. It's a slight miserable thing of a nod, like a half-dead swallow trying to find its wings. "I need a place to sleep."

"Everything all right?"

She nods again.

"How'd you get here?"

"Walked. It ain't far."

Rory sets the stick back under his bed. "Pike know you're here?"

She shakes her head. "He's hunting."

"Hunting? Where?"

"I don't know. Out in the mountains somewhere. He's been hunting since y'all came back. He don't sleep anymore. Can I stay?"

"I guess so." Rory finds his jeans beside the bed and pulls them on under his covers. "You don't think Pike'll get mad when he gets in, do you?"

"No." She pulls off her gloves. "I left him a note. Besides he told me to come over here if I ever needed to."

"All right. Sit tight and I'll stoke up the fire and get you some blankets or something."

She sits on the floor and unbundles Monster from somewhere in her clothes. Rory pulls an extra blanket from under his bed and sets her up a pallet three or four feet off from the stove. He opens the stove and throws a log in and stokes up the fire. "Do you roll around a lot in your sleep?"

She turns her face up to him. Monster curled in her lap, licking the tips of her fingers.

"I don't want you accidentally running up against the stove. If you roll around in your sleep, I'll take the floor and you can have the bed. I'd let you have the bed anyway, but the sheets ain't clean and I only got the one set."

"I'll be fine. Thank you."

"Okay."

Rory sits on his bed, watching her and Monster snuggle into the bedding, making sure she doesn't move any closer to the fire. It never occurring to him it might be impolite to watch. When he sees her situated, he finds his pills on the windowsill and leans against the wall with his knobby legs pulled up to shield the bottom half of his face and dryswallows four of them.

"What are those for?"

He holds up his bruised hand, flexing it so she can see the uneven bones. He raises his left arm, displaying four long finger welts down his bicep. He turns his torso to show a set of fist sized bruises splotching his back like tumors. He forcibly straightens his left leg, the gristle and bone popping like cherry bombs.

"Can I have one?"

"Not without Pike's say-so."

She strokes Monster. He's nestled into her thin chest, already asleep and shuddering slightly, his fur blanched and silvery in the moonlight. "It's a strange hobby. The fighting."

"It won't always be a hobby."

"What'll it be?"

"There's a contest in Toledo. You fight everyone who shows up and the last one standing wins ten thousand dollars. I'm gonna win that and find a boxing trainer somewhere."

"I believe you will." She closes her eyes. "Thank you, Rory."

"Anytime."

She's asleep in minutes. Rory finds his glass of water and drinks it. Then he stands and finds his dumbbells in the dark, and places them between her and the stove. He looks down at her and her face is like a piece of polished bone in the bleak moonlight. Monster's eyes open, sparking, and his jaw yawns, exposing his vicious little pricks.

CHAPTER 57

*~ As though it has to pass through a very
dirty windowpane to reach him. ~*

Later that night, the meadow across from Rory's cabin. The night air chill and dangerous, as sharp as a cat's tooth. The stars bursting like frozen collisions against the black of the night, and the moon full and brittle white, like a disk of ice, as though you could breathe on it and melt it into the dark. Rory lies in the middle of the meadow, his head propped on a log, his eyes drifting across the firmament. It's all blending together again in his memory. A man lying face down in the mud and dust, his back a grisly hole of bone shards and meat. The chemical heroin and cum stench that ran off Dana. And his sister. There's still the same feeling he's ever had for her, but it's dimmed, as though it has to pass through a very dirty windowpane to reach him.

Exhaustion. Tired of fighting in the bar and tired of working out. Ready to lose and be done with this car-crash of a dream. Ready to ask a girl out. It's been years since he had a girl, it sticks in him like a cancer. It's why he's out here in the meadow, instead of inside. It's been so long since he was in the same room alone with a girl, he couldn't find anyway to get to sleep. Rory closes his eyes, let's his mind drift. It doesn't drift far from familiar ground.

There was a barn with the honeysuckle vines growing up the side, bare in the winter. The piercing voices of his parents, drinking hard after his sister died. The nightly chores, emptying the slop bucket into the pig trough. Then hunkering down in his work jacket like a turtle hunkering into its shell, breathing warm air into his hands, waiting for their shrill hatred to thin out of the house.

It never did seem to. Not all the way. It hung in the air like smoke from a wood stove fire started with the flue closed.

Then his mother. Then his father.

CHAPTER 58

~ There are some things AA doesn't cover. ~

Rory dug the key out from under the rock and opened the door. The late summer sunlight was still strong, flooding over the great room in buckets of light and warmth. His father sat at the table, a whiskey bottle by his elbow. He'd been drinking every night after Rory went to bed. There are some things AA doesn't cover. Fire being one.

"The Sawyers will be here in about an hour," his father said. "You can wait out front."

"Why?"

"To pick you up. For the weekend."

"I don't want to."

"I know it. But I need time to gather my thoughts."

"I won't bother you."

His father pulled a filterless cigarette out of the pack on the table and tapped it on his lighter to settle the tobacco. Then he stuck it in his mouth.

"I'll stay in my room."

"Sorry, bud."

Rory looked at the old man. His face was thin and worked over. He lit the cigarette, his cigarette hand missing the two fingers from a chainsaw accident. Smoke curled around his face like a query mark as he puffed it to life. "I miss them as bad as you do," Rory said.

His father's eyes were hazel and flecked with dead light. "I know it."

Rory never had nothing to say to that. His father touched his hand then chucked his chin towards the door for him to wait outside. So he did.

All of them, they're like people somebody told him about. A dream is a sausage mill you feed your life into. The night as chill as a little girl's teeth. Nothing changes. Ever.

CHAPTER 59

~ That's various of you. ~

Pike trades half the meat to a local pig farmer in exchange for doing the butchering and drives home. For the first time in weeks he feels steady on his feet, like he's regained his sea legs after too long a period ashore. Then he opens the door to his apartment and finds Wendy, cross-legged on the floor, smoking a cigarette, reading Poe, and his steadiness doesn't feel so steady. He fakes it.

She closes the book. "Rory says you're such the reader. How come you don't own no books?"

Pike shuts the door and walks to the window and cracks it, letting her smoke escape. "I get them out of the library."

"What's the last book you read then?"

"It was about Sand Creek." He sits on the bed.

"What's Sand Creek?"

"It's a place in Colorado."

"What about before that?"

"*Beowulf.*"

"That's various of you."

"Not really."

She wipes her nose on the back of her hand. "I need to ask you a question." Her voice is hard.

A loose stream of cold air from the window slicks along the floorboards and slithers up his legs. "I didn't find out anything you don't know," he answers.

Her sharp chin bobs up and down. "I'm sorry I spit on you," she says. "And I'm sorry I haven't been talking to you."

"You're under no obligation to talk to anybody you don't want to. That includes me."

"I know what kind of mom she was. But." Her chin furrows unsteadily. "I don't know how to say it."

Pike leans forward and puts his hands together in a double fist in front of his mouth. "I let your mom down when she was even younger than you. I had to know how bad."

She looks down at the floor and he can't see anything but the top of her head. "Why did you let her down?"

"I don't know the answer to that. Anything I told you would be a lie."

"You didn't want her? As a kid?"

"That wasn't it," Pike says. "I always loved her as much as I was able. I just wasn't very able."

Another cold stream of air. And it seems to touch Wendy. She shudders, and then sets her muscles to stop herself from shuddering. "I'm sick of it. I'm so sick of the whole thing it makes me want to walk through a window."

"I know it." The air in the room hangs over them like a wet canvas. He stands. "Will you take a drive with me?"

She nods. And makes it all the way down to the truck without letting him see her face.

CHAPTER 60

*~ As though they're surfacing from the
black depths of an ocean. ~*

They drive back into the mountains. And they keep driving. The day darkens with winter clouds and the sun falls and the clouds clear and there's the purple twilight, falling down on them like a new kind of snow. The truck winds through the mountains like an undercurrent through the ocean. Pike talks while they drive, pointing out the mountains and hollows that he knows the names of, telling every story he can think of about the people that live in them. He tells her what the land will look like when spring comes. How green it'll get. Then he tells her how when he was out west he thought he'd forgotten the color of green altogether. He doesn't tell her that he didn't mind in the least.

Then they stop at a store and buy two Cokes and a fresh pack of cigarettes and they continue driving. Smoking silently and drinking the Cokes. Listening to country music on the radio and watching the stars appear, one by one, across the vault. Pike turns off the headlights and they drive mountaintop to mountaintop by starlight. The low clouds wisping beneath the stars above them, then over the ravines below as they climb. At times the mountains are no longer there at all. Nor the truck, nor even each other. Nothing but the sky and the stars glinting coldly, then growing and warming as they rise up to meet them, as though they're surfacing from the black depths of an ocean. And then they're within them, the stars whirling around them as though they're the lynchpin on which the firmament revolves.

And then they descend again. Diving into the blackness of the gorge below again.

CHAPTER 61

~ That kind ends up dead every time. ~

The reverend leaves the house twice every Saturday. Once in the morning for groceries at a boutique market with his oldest daughter, once in the afternoon for a cigar and coffee at a corner tobacco shop. He doesn't live with his constituents, this spokesman for his oppressed brothers. There ain't no boutique grocery stores downtown. You can't even see Over-the-Rhine from his oversized Victorian in Mount Adams.

It's Saturday afternoon. The sun's thin and washed out behind the clouds. Derrick won't do what he's going to do in front of the man's daughter. The reverend walks with his shoulders back and his head erect, his round brown face like a polished black walnut bust above his immaculate suit. It's never just a walk, never just a cigar. It's a visitation.

Derrick pulls alongside him and reaches over and pops the passenger side door. "Get in."

The reverend raises an eyebrow, continues walking. "This is not one of your wiser moves, son," he says without looking at Derrick.

"Maybe. But it wasn't a fucking request. Get in."

The reverend stops walking. Stands, looking up at the sky. Then he eases his large frame into the car, smoothing down his overcoat. Derrick stomps the gas and the Monte Carlo waffles out into the street, peels down the hill. "You ever call me son again I'll shoot you in the face," Derrick says.

"Am I to expect anything different?"

"We'll see how you behave. Boy."

The reverend laughs out loud. "You've come to deal?"

"Maybe."

"You didn't seem so interested in dealing the other night, when you met with Dick Fleischer."

"Fleischer's a sack of shit. I don't deal with shit."

"I see."

Derrick slips the car off the road, into a small lot by the Ohio, at the foot of Mount Adams. "I'm a good cop."

"You and I have different ideas of what it means to be a good cop, I think."

"Drug wars don't happen where I am. Kids don't get shot."

"Unless you shoot them. You're a thug, Kreiger. And you're corrupt."

"Hell, at least the people I get, they've done something worth being got for. That little nigger I shot with his six-year-old sister in the hospital. Thirteen hours of surgery. That shit doesn't happen, not on my watch."

"It's an obsession with you?"

"The rest we can compromise on. You can have a say in how cop work is done in Over-the-Rhine."

"So we are dealing?"

"You won't ever get this kind of deal again."

"But only on your say-so, Derrick. Am I right? You reserve the right to pass judgment as you see fit?"

"Just with that one thing. That kind ends up dead every time. I don't compromise on that."

The reverend looks Derrick over. "Lord, what I wouldn't give to be a fly on your therapist's wall."

"We got a deal?"

"Perhaps." The reverend nods to himself, thinking. "What exactly am I supposed to gain from the arrangement?"

"I done told you. You get a say in how the neighborhood's policed."

"A say?"

"A say. I'm a damn sight better than the helicopters and the SWAT teams. That's what's next, an occupation."

"I'm not sure you're better."

"You know I am. I live in Over-the-Rhine. It matters to me. Your alternative is mass arrests and submachine guns. The kind of shit that's starting in L.A. and New York. I'm corrupt, you say, but I'm a hell of a lot better than what's clean."

The reverend stares out the window. "I obviously can't support you. Not publicly."

"You don't have to. You don't even have to quit condemning me, not immediately. You just have to let the chief know you're thinking about finding other shit to focus on, and find something."

"There can't be any way of it blowing back on me. You can't be crooked, Kreiger. Not in any way that matters."

"There won't be no loose ends, not when I'm done." Derrick sticks his hand out. "Shake it."

The reverend shakes his hand. And laughs. First in a long slow rumble, then in a full guffaw. Then he wipes his eyes. "I'm dealing with the devil."

Derrick shifts the car into drive. "You won't get a better deal anywhere else."

CHAPTER 62

~ There are places you can still be what you are. ~

The sun sets with a final bath of light that runs like warm water down the Nanticote street, rinsing the row of houses in shadow and resting on the last, a two story Colonial. Inside the four of them eat beneath a huge and dusty chandelier. Pike finishes first and crosses his knife and fork on his plate and looks around the table. It's a hell of a meal. Venison roast and venison strips and fried liver and onions, all of which he and Iris spent the better part of the day preparing.

He watches Wendy. She chews delicately, her left hand folded demurely in her lap. She's wearing the first dress Pike has ever seen her in. She got it from the thrift store. It's black and high-necked and patched all over, but it fits her. Perfectly. She's only been a couple months in Nanticonte but it looks like years on her. She's shedding her girlishness, her pretty white face leaning out, her thin hands losing the awkwardness she carried from Cincinnati.

Then there's Rory. Slumped back in his chair, hunched to one side like his body's been thrown off kilter and he can't muster the strength to regain his equilibrium. Picking at his food like an automaton, his effortless grace having fled him, left him a lumbering shell of his former self. He needs out of here. Somewhere he can flex and move, where the locals can't keep you pinned down with their shitty little renditions of you. There are places you can still be what you are.

After dinner, Pike stands outside the back door, smoking and watching the kitchen light spill out the windows, burnishing the snow banks a fluttering bronze. Listening to Wendy and Rory bicker over the cleanup.

The door opens and Iris steps out. "Sorry to make you smoke outside."

"It's your house."

"Jack wouldn't let me smoke inside." She pulls a Marlboro Light out of her flannel shirt pocket and lights it with a match, her hands shaking in the cold. "Even in my own house I keep on coming out in the cold. Stupid, ain't it?"

"I don't mind."

She draws on her cigarette and folds her arms across her breast. Then shudders as if suddenly struck by the chill air.

"How are you holding up?"

"You know. I'm lonesome. But I've been lonesome for a long time."

"It ain't none of my business. But he wants you to come back."

"You're right, it ain't none of your business. And it wouldn't matter if I went back or not." Iris shakes her head, smoke spilling out of her mouth like water from a shaken glass. "He's not sheriff because he needs the job. He's got plenty of money from the real estate. He's sheriff for the lousiest reason I can think of. His grandfather was sheriff before his father, and he thinks he'd be betraying his father's memory if he was anything else. It's nothing but second-rate family history. Makes me mad enough to twist his little prick off."

"I never expected it would be any other way."

"Yeah. Well. Jack never wanted to be a cop, and I never wanted to be married to a cop. Cops turn strange. They end up spending most of their energy hammering their personalities into cop molds. Jack used to have plans for his life."

"Most of us did," Pike says. "Before we became what we are."

"Well. There you go, then. It's a fucking tragedy all over, ain't it?"

CHAPTER 63

~ I earn twenty-five dollars a day. And expenses. ~

Black snow and exhaust fumes. A gang of lanky-haired children picking like magpies through the oily rocks for anything that shines. Derrick strolls from his car to the first fire pit under the train bridge. He doesn't bother to zip up his leather jacket, letting his Colt .45 hang out. He's spent the whole day running down pimps and dealers, wising them up to his ability to be in all places at once. He doesn't want anyone thinking he's out of touch. Sooner or later somebody will be asking questions. He ain't planning on leaving a single motherfucker in town who doesn't understand the consequences if they answer. And he's almost done. Dana's the last name on his list.

Two men just under the bridge. One a scruffy black junky with red eyes and a shoulder length Jheri curl, the other a wiry white kid with sandy blonde hair. Derrick gets within two paces of them and pulls his .45 and holds it at his side.

"There really ain't no need for you to pull your piece." The junky's voice is even and chastising, like he's hipping Derrick to some piece of etiquette he might not have known about.

"I'm looking for a hooker named Dana," Derrick says. "Point me at whatever nigger she's under."

"Whatever nigger?" The junky's eyes fire black with hatred. "I don't know any niggers."

Derrick reaches in his back pocket, flips out his shield, lets them ogle it. "Get smart with me again and I'll put two in your nigger ass."

"I know you." A flush shades the corners of the blonde kid's rawboned face, excited with himself at the thought of knowing anything.

"How the fuck do you know me, boy?"

"I seen your picture. Seen you in the papers." He slaps out his hand. "Name's Bogie."

"Put your fucking hand away, boy, before I stuff it down your throat."

Bogie shrugs like that's happened before and doesn't scare him in the least. "Dana ain't been here in days. You was right, though. The last time anyone saw her she got dragged out from under a nigger. Want to know what happened to him?"

"Boy, you are testing my patience."

"Shot." Bogie nods his head at one of the campfires staggered around the shantytown. "Right there. Real big gun too. Blew a hole in his chest I could have stuck my head in."

"You saw it?"

"Fuck no. I got here late. His body was still there, though. Ass naked from the waist down. These ratty motherfuckers had already stoled his pants. Underwear too, if he was wearing any."

"Who shot him?"

"That's a negotiating question. You got to throw an offer out with it."

The .45 roars in Derrick's hand, the slug ripping past Bogie's ear, clanging off an iron beam five foot behind his head. Bogie doesn't even look at the gun. "You got a cigarette on you?"

Derrick can't help but grin. He drops the muzzle of the .45 and fingers a Marlboro red out of his shirt pocket and tosses it to Bogie. "You're a cool little fucker."

Bogie cups a hand around the cigarette and lights it with a grimy book of matches. "Ain't cool at all. I just seen too much of your horse-shit lately for it to bother me much."

Derrick palms a five out of his billfold, drops it fluttering at the kid's feet. "That's it for negotiations."

"That'll do." Bogie crouches to pick up the bill. "He was a big briar. Called himself Pike. Had a boy wonder with him that went by Rory."

Derrick's head swarms with blood, a thick heart pump surging like a swollen river over a low dam. "Why?"

Bogie clears his throat meaningfully, his eyes flit down to the bill in his hand.

Derrick lifts the .45, one-handed. Puts the front sight on Bogie's forehead. "Don't make me tell you again. We're done negotiating."

"They was looking for Dana. Like you."

"Where is she?" Derrick's voice sounds like ashes being scraped out of a metal bucket.

"Don't know. But if you're still in a negotiating mood, I bet I can find out."

Derrick pulls the trigger back. Just a little, to the point where it catches before breaking.

"I'll bet they damn near scared her clean. And I know where she goes when she wants to get clean." Bogie grins a loose grin. "I'm a regular motherfucking gumshoe, though. I earn twenty-five dollars a day. And expenses."

CHAPTER 64

~ Rory folds his hands in front of his face, tries a chuckle. ~

Rory stands in his doorway, toweling sweat off his shaved neck. "It's a beautiful morning, Pike. What the hell're you doing in it?"

Pike hands him a Styrofoam cup. "Brought coffee." Rory watches him take a seat at the writing table and pull his gloves off in a soft Vicodin blur. Pike gestures at the bed. "Take a seat."

Rory obeys, dabbing at his shoulders with the towel.

"You high?" Pike asks.

Rory tosses the towel on the floor and takes a slug off the coffee, scalding his tongue. But he barely notices. "My hand was hurting."

Pike nods, slowly. The snow is melting of the roof, the water tip-tip-tip-tapping on the ground outside. Rory can see the drops falling through his window. The sun is pouring into the cabin in a easy wave. "I owe you an apology," Pike says. He uses his middle finger to adjust his glasses on his nose. "I came here to give it."

"What for?"

"For taking you with me to Cincinnati."

Rory leans forward, rests his elbows on his knees. "I'd do it again."

"I know it."

Rory folds his hands in front of his face, tries a chuckle. It comes out weak. "It won't be a trip I'll forget anytime soon."

Pike sets his coffee cup on the floor. "Say anything you need to say. I'll listen."

"Will it help?"

"No."

"Should I even ask why it don't seem to bother you none?"

"I know some things you don't."

"Like?"

"If the winds rage, doth not the sea wax mad?"

Rory throws his towel at Pike, who catches it. "Don't quote at me."

Pike looks at him steadily. "What we did had to be done. We didn't have any choice about it. Compared to some of the things that get done that don't have to be done, we come up pretty light on the scale."

Rory's thoughts catch and stall like an overloaded engine. "We had to kill him? That black guy with the hooker?"

"Yep."

"You don't know as he would've got me with that knife."

"Sure I do. As soon as we turned around if nothing else. He was morally yellow. He was exactly what it looked like he was. Like Derrick."

"You can spot them?"

"I wouldn't have shot him if I couldn't."

"You're a scary motherfucker."

"No," Pike says. "I just know what scary looks like. You could work on it yourself."

"I don't think I'm ready to be you."

"I ain't telling you to be. I'm telling you that you're all over the place, and you need to get your shit together. Part of that is learning how to see. Right now, you're the kind of kid that'd show up at a knife fight bare-fisted."

Rory covers his face with his hands. "Jesus," he says again. "I never have any fucking idea what to say when I'm talking to you."

"That's my point," Pike says. "Owning your own words is a good place to start. What you do and say, that's what you are."

Rory's face is still in his hands.

"Take all the time off you need. I'll pay you. If you need anything else, let me know. I'll do whatever I can."

"Why did you come back?" Rory drops his hands and looks at Pike. "Here. To Kentucky. And where the hell did you go when you left? You could tell me that. Telling me something about yourself that made any kind of sense might make me feel a whole hell of a lot better."

"I went all over, but I ended up in Mexico," Pike says, with no hesitation. "I worked for a coyote named Joaquin. He managed a tunnel from Juárez into the basement of an El Paso safehouse. I was one of his drivers. It was my job to pick up the illegals and get them to their jobsites in the back of my truck."

"So why'd you came back? You wised up and got sick of it?"

"Not hardly. Joaquin was scared shitless the illegals would rip him off, use the tunnel for free. So he had it built with locks on the tunnel door and a basement like a bomb shelter into the El Paso house. When he got a load in there, he'd lock them up and call one of us. It was our job to get there quick, before the air ran out." Pike lights a cigarette and stares into his smoke. "One day he called to tell me he'd let a group through the day before and hadn't been able to call anyone. He told me to check on them, but at this point I could probably take my time. There was a girl in the group named Guillermina. I knew her."

"Jesus." Rory stares at him. "What'd you do?"

"I went to his house. His wife had had a heart attack the day before, which is why he hadn't called me. They'd been at the hospital the whole day."

"And?"

"And I shot them both."

"Both of them?" Rory asks. "His wife too?"

"I don't regret that. She lived well off of what he did."

"So did you."

"That's the answer to what you asked. It's why I came back."

Rory nods. Then starts laughing. And laughs until his eyes water, until his nose runs. He wipes it on the back of his hand. "I'll be damned. That didn't help at all."

CHAPTER 65

~ Derrick grins the kind of grin that makes
his pacemaker work double time. ~

Dana's mother spits smoke out of her cigarette like the thought of her daughter has curdled the tobacco. "The Cleveland Roadside Motel in Hamilton. She called me last night looking for money." Her breath is two parts gin.

Derrick replaces his badge into his pocket. She'd never even looked at it. "What else did she say?"

"That she needed the money to buy a bus ticket. That she'd made a mistake and there was a man after her. That she needed to find her way out of town." She waves her cigarette across her chest in dismissal. "It's the sort of thing you surely hear from these women all the time."

"You don't believe her?"

"Of course I believe her. In her life it all sounds perfectly plausible. I just don't want to be involved in it."

Derrick grins the kind of grin that makes his pacemaker work double time. "What if I'm the man she's talking about?"

"Then I suppose you'll have at her. If it's not you, it'll be someone. That's not in doubt."

Derrick digs a business card out of his breast pocket, holds it out to her. It has a fake name on it, the same name as the badge he showed her. "Will you be home for the next couple days?"

She sips from her gin glass, taking the card without looking at it, swaying slightly like a heat wave rising off a highway. "I have nowhere else to be."

CHAPTER 66

~ *I don't know as I'd follow her.* ~

Rory's been wanting a tough one. One of the local rednecks with a face like a pork chop. For a minute he thought he'd lucked out, too. The kid stepped in the ring, built like a linebacker, the biggest yet. But he's nothing. Slow, with a fat face that makes a good target, advertising every punch with a flick of his eyes in the direction he's swinging. One of the college boys by the ring cups his mouth, "KILL THAT INBRED MOTHERFUCKER!"

"I'll make him squeal like a pig," Linebacker says over his shoulder. To prove it, he hauls off with a heavy right lead.

Rory's floating on Vicodin. He tucks his chin, lets the blow slide off his forehead, counters with a left hook that flattens Linebacker's nose, breaking it. Linebacker tries to throw another right lead. Rory heaves up his arm, blocks it, pins Linebacker's nose again in the same spot. Then he clinches him. "I ain't gonna knock you down," he says into Linebacker's ear.

Linebacker pushes him away, wipes blood across his glove. "You can't knock me down, faggot."

Hate falls over Rory like a drop cloth. "Sure I can." He hooks him in the gut, follows with a bone crushing straight lead, disintegrating his nose. "But you're gonna give up standing."

"Fuck you." Linebacker spits blood, tries a weak one two combination. Rory slaps both punches down and fixes a straight left into the kid's nose. He twists his glove on it. Cartilage crackles, grinds against the bone underneath like he's grinding his fist in gravel. The blood drains out of Linebacker's face. He swallows.

"Sick, ain't it?" Rory says, grinning. Linebacker sways, holding one glove over his face, the other lilting at his side. Rory drills him in the nose again. Rotating his glove, using his fist as a pestle. Linebacker drops to one knee and pukes. Prodigiously. A frothy sloshing wave of beer and chili. Then he collapses on all fours, shooting a furious wet look at Rory before puking again.

"That's what I meant," Rory says over him. "You ain't hurt bad enough you couldn't still fight, but I'll bet you don't."

He doesn't.

"Jesus," the ring announcer says. Then skitters out of the way as Rory moves to exit the ring.

Rory stalks to the table. He doesn't sit down. "I'm sick of them motherfuckers."

"It showed," Pike says.

"I saw it, too," Wendy agrees.

Rory's jaw clenches, relaxes, clenches again. His shoulders tight, rippling under his shirt. He hangs his head and massages the knuckles of his left hand, staring barely restrained rage into the floor.

"Sit down," Pike says.

"I'll stand."

"You'll sit." Pike says, and something in his voice turns Rory's knees into water, so he sits. Pike's hand grips his shoulder and squeezes. Rory closes his eyes, wanting to mist away into the barsmoke.

"You two need anything?"

Rory's eyes snap open at the waitress. "Bourbon. Double. With a beer back."

"Getting drunk ain't a bad idea," Pike says, after the waitress has walked away.

"That's good. I plan on it." Rory reaches down in his shorts pocket, fumbles up a fistful of pills. He palms them into his mouth.

The waitress returns with the bourbon and the beer. Pike hands her a bill before Rory can find his money. "Two more bourbons. And another beer back."

"Whatever you say."

Rory downs his bourbon and waits. The liquor hits the pills, a wave of nausea makes his eyes unfocus. He lets his head hang back on his neck and stares at the crossbeams in the ceiling. He drains his beer without once lowering his head. There's a slide guitar somewhere in the background, floating out of the jukebox. It's long and sad. It sheds him like water, leaving a hollow feeling in its place.

The waitress returns with the drinks. Pike pays her and slides them across the table to Rory. "There's an extra bourbon in there," the waitress says. "It's from an admirer."

Rory drinks it.

"You wanna know who she is?" the waitress asks.

"Nope."

"Right there." The waitress nods across the room at a blonde girl in a fleece-lined jacket, smoking a cigarette at the bar. "She wants to say something to you. I'll go get her."

Rory looks up to stop her, but she's already gone, speaking to the blonde. Then the blonde's there in front of them. She's thin and pretty, her eyes are a little reddened by beer. Two other girls who look just like her are standing by the bar, grinning the kind of grin that usually indicates some kind of brain damage. "I know you," she says. "Your name's Rory."

Rory looks at her.

"I went to high school with you. Used to sit right across from you in English. You even went out with my sister."

Rory looks away from her. Up at the ceiling. Then back, and she's still standing there. "And?"

"And nothing really. I wanted to say hello."

"Well. You did."

"Yeah, I guess I did." She turns to the bar. And stops. She turns back to Rory. "You know, we were all real sorry. About what happened. We'd have told you that but you were gone."

"I bet you could've gone without saying it altogether, if you'd tried a little harder."

"I'm sorry," she says, and walks away.

A scowl crosses Wendy's face, like a flock of geese blacking out the sun. "You're a fucking idiot."

Rory looks at her in surprise. "Me?"

She leans way forward over the table and picks up his empty beer bottle. She flips it once in the air, catches it by the neck, and hurtles at him. His head ticks sideways like it's set on a spring and the bottle whips past him. He hears a clunking smash and turns to watch a brunette in tight jeans collapse, blood spritzing from her head like it's a plugged sprinkler. A fresh-faced girl screams and drops to her knees, smacking at the blood like she's trying to slap out a fire.

Rory turns wide-eyed back to Wendy. Or where Wendy had been. "What was that?" he says to Pike. Pike shrugs his shoulders, a look of honest confusion on his face. Rory blinks and wipes his hand down the side of his face where the bottle would've hit. He feels halfway sober all the sudden. "Where'd she go?"

Pike flicks his eyes at a side door used for loading music equipment. "Though I'd say she needs a minute."

CHAPTER 67

~ Tuning himself up for what's to come. ~

*T*he motel's a roadside shitpile outside the Hamilton city limits. Ten powder blue units surrounding a paved cul-de-sac, birdshit spattered, the snow melting in filthy streaks down the siding. Derrick buys a Coke and a candy bar from a vending machine by the office and hunkers down on his heels to eat, his eyes on the one car in the lot besides his. A rust-colored Volkswagen beetle, strangle crumpled around the middle like its been rolled sideways down a hill.

The candy bar is the first food he's had in two days. It's dirt in his mouth and he has to force-swallow it. But he knows he won't be eating for a long time afterwards. Lightning from a far-off storm plays over the dismal snow-covered plains. Nobody passes the hotel on the highway and nobody enters or exits any of the hotel rooms. The only other soul around is Bogie, asleep in the Monte Carlo. His head leaned back in his seat, his mouth moving as though he's singing to himself.

The lightning plays out. There's a lull and it starts again, this time closer to the hotel. There's been no sleep lately. The lightning flashes behind Derrick's eyes, thudding at the base of his brainstem. It reaches down and clutches his heart, forces it to dance to its measure. Derrick drops the candy bar wrapper from his limp fingers and stands creakily. Tuning himself up for what's to come.

Then he's finished with the candy bar. He walks in the hotel office and flashes a badge at the pimply flat-headed kid behind the counter. "Dana Jennings."

The kid's head is a long blood-sausage, his chin blending with his neck in a mass of fat. He holds up three fingers without looking up from his magazine, like this is a question he answers to cops three or four times a day.

CHAPTER 68

~ Her lips are bloodstains against the white of her skin. ~

Rory finds her in the side alley. Squatting on the concrete stoop in front of the kitchen door, smoking a cigarette. The smell of wet snow and exhaust. Street lights bleeding all over the wet blacktop. She turns as Rory sits so that he's facing the back of her head. He stuffs his hands in his sweatshirt and clears his throat. The back of her head bobs slightly as she pulls smoke off the cigarette. One of Pike's Pall Malls, the size of a small tree in her skinny fingers. "You probably shouldn't be smoking," Rory says.

"You probably shouldn't be a fucking idiot."

He swallows and breathes in the cold air. It's sweet and thick, flavored of bourbon. "I was blowing off steam."

"I don't give a shit about your steam."

He rolls his shoulders and winces at a shooting twinge at the top of the rotation. He's having trouble focusing. Wendy flips her cigarette in a red spark that ends in a sizzling collision with a snowdrift. Rory thinks seriously. Tries to, anyway. "I guess I don't know what I'm supposed to say."

She turns to face him, the whites of her eyes shot through with red like gunpowder sparks, her mouth like a bloodstain against the white of her skin. He reaches out and knuckles her tear wet cheek. She smacks his hand back. "You're a fucking idiot." She kicks at the snow and moves to turn her head away from him.

But he doesn't let her.

CHAPTER 69

~ Prying her open, exposing her like an oyster. ~

Derrick covers the hotel door's peephole with a grimy thumb and knocks. He doesn't expect her to answer, but she does. And when she sees him she tries to whip the door closed, but Derrick jams his foot in and drops his shoulder, pounds it wide open. She spills backwards onto the greasy gray carpet and he slaps the door shut behind him. She scuttles to her knees and wraps her arms around his thighs, wearing a long white T-shirt and nothing else. Derrick looks down into her matted brown hair, the strangely tender whiteness of her scalp, feels the resolution he's so carefully formed start to slip. He puts his hand under her chin and pulls her face up gently. "It's okay," he says. "I just have questions."

She takes his hand and runs it down her slimy tear-slicked cheek. He's never seen her without makeup. He lifts her to her feet and leads her to the bed and sits her down. He hunches on his boot heels in front of her and lights a Marlboro. He sticks it between her pale lips.

"They shot a john," she snuffles. "Shot him dead right in front of everybody. Then kidnapped me. Nobody will touch me anymore. I had to get away before somebody hurt me."

"Relax." Derrick puts a hand around her head and massages the back of her neck. "I only need to know what you told them. About me."

"Nothing." A wave of tremors ripples from her cigarette hand all the way up her arm. The loose skin on her face flaps like a battered flag in a hurricane wind. "Nothing much. Nothing worth worrying about."

"What?"

"I told them you didn't kill Sarah." She sniffles and lifts the hem of her T-shirt to wipe her nose. "I told them she died of an overdose. But they thought you'd killed her. The big one wanted to think it, anyway." She makes a sound that could be sandpaper being dragged down an iron bar, or a chuckle. For a second the old Dana's back, her face as dull and vengeful as a spent shell casing. "I made sure to tell him different."

"And that's all you told them?"

Her eyes skid away from his face. "Yeah."

He takes her jaw firmly. "What else?"

"You're not gonna hurt me?"

He pats her naked knee with his free hand, exhaustion and nausea washing over him like a chemical bath. Prying her open, exposing her like an oyster. Seeing all the way down to her quivering core. "I get nothing out of hurting you."

Her eyes swim. Broad and open on his. "They already knew about Sarah. That you kept an eye out for her. That you and her knew each other." Her face squirms in his hand and knows he's squeezing too hard, but he doesn't stop. He's not entirely sure he can. "Please," she says through compressed lips, her voice rising and crackling like a piece of old-growth timber bent to its breaking point. He lets go, she melts in a cascade of tears. He takes the cigarette from her, drops it on the carpet, wraps an arm around her neck. Pulls her face into his chest.

Derrick had figured she'd know what's coming next, but she fights like she doesn't. Her fingers scramble for his eyes as jerks her hair back, and pounds his brass knuckles into her forehead. Her skull crumbles like chalk and her eyes glass over, then flush with blood. Derrick cocks his fist for the next blow and her hands slap at his fist. He hammers her temple with the side of the knuckles, like he's driving a nail. Her eyes blank, and she's dead. Derrick stands, breathing heavily, his fingers aching at the joints. One down.

A knock on the door. Peephole. Speak of the devil. Derrick slides his knuckles back in his jeans pocket. He slips his tactical knife out of his pocket, flicks out the blade. "C'mon, motherfucker," Bogie wheedles through the door, "I need to take a piss. That cocksucker in the office won't let me use his bathroom. Says I'm dirty. The next motherfucker who says I'm dirty is getting an asswhipping. You ask anybody."

Derrick swings the door open, not wide enough to give him a view of the room. Bogie swaggers in and heads for the bathroom door, his shoulders and hips sashaying side to side. Then he sees Dana's body, crumpled against the bed. He turns, his eyes wide, his mouth in an idiot O.

It's taken something out of Derrick, killing Dana. His hands are weak. It's like he's broken a small piece of himself in two, a very small piece he keeps buried way back under his sternum. But he focuses and flashes his blade across Bogie's neck. It snags, tears, rips a gash across his throat that all but decapitates him. Derrick shoves the kid backwards and his corpse hits the bed, spurting blood.

CHAPTER 70

~ Jack puts his hands on hips and stares
up at the streetlight for a while. ~

Pike waits for Rory and Wendy to return, letting his mind wander. When it wanders a little further than he likes, he signals the waitress and orders a bourbon and a Coke.

Then spends a long time staring at them.

Then drinks the bourbon.

Wendy comes in sometime after that. Alone. She stands in front of the table and waits for Pike to pull on his coat, flushed and working to slow her breathing. They don't talk for a long time on the walk home. Then Pike can't not talk anymore. "Rory's one of the best friends I have," he starts.

Her eyes flicker over at him, showing nothing. "He's the only friend you have."

"I'm not sure what to say here," he says, standing. "I was hoping you'd help."

She grins up at him, her face lit and shadowed like a kerosene lantern. "You don't need to say anything," she says, and her laugh warbles shrilly.

They walk home the rest of the way in silence. And she goes to bed. But Pike can't sleep, and he can't take being indoors with her. So he takes his cigarettes and stands out front of the building, leaning on the front door, staring out into the night.

He's not sure he'll ever sleep again. Thinking of Wendy's grandmother, thinking of Wendy, trying to come up with more objections than he's able. Rory's a good kid, as good as he's ever known. Wendy will never know what Rory's done for her, but Pike does. The Cincinnati trip's eating into him, and maybe Wendy can take the edge off of some of it. She's young, no doubt about it, but he's known younger to start seeing men, to get married even. Both in Mexico and here in Kentucky. No matter how young she is, she'd be treated better than any woman Pike's ever been with.

A man stumbles from streetlamp to streetlamp towards him, as though gutshot and staggering wildly for home. Pike flicks flame on a Pall Mall and grins as the man passes directly under a streetlamp. It's Jack, lurching down the sidewalk, a half empty bottle of Old Crow swaying in his right hand for ballast. He sees Pike and somehow makes it over to stand in front of him.

Pike nods. "Jack."

Jack's eyes are pinched and his mustache is singed as though he's fallen face first into a bonfire. "Pike." He fumbles for his mustache and strokes it.

"Having a night out?"

He nods. "Having a drink."

Pike smokes his cigarette and lets Jack figure out what it is he wants to say.

"There's a woman I see sometimes. She lives back thataway." Jack speaks slowly, as though he can only release each words after careful inspection. "I've been drinking for awhile, I started this morning at the office."

"Well. You ain't hurting anybody."

"I don't guess I am."

"You look like you could use some sleep."

Jack raises the bottle up at the streetlight and eyes the contents. "I've been sleeping at the office. Right now I don't much want to be anywhere I've been for too long."

"Spent my whole life with that feeling."

"You know I ain't even took down the pictures my father hung on the walls? Never even bothered to change them."

"They're just pictures."

"They probably are. But there's a meaning in it too." He spins the lid off the bottle, drinks, spins it back on. "It'd be easier probably if Iris and I had kids. Could've hung their pictures up."

"Could just as well have turned out the same."

Jack coughs into his hand. "I don't give a shit about this other girl.

It was like the office, I wanted to be around somebody that I hadn't been around too long."

"There's worse reasons."

Jack puts his hands on hips and stares up at the streetlight for a while. "I miss her, Pike."

"Why don't I drive you over to the hotel? Get you a room, let you sleep it off?"

Jack nods. For a long time. "That's probably a good idea," he says.

CHAPTER 71

~ The backs of their heads a wall to the world around them. ~

Derrick grinds gears, pounds the gas. The Monte Carlo burns down the highway like the engine block's spitting fire, rolling and rattling like a Gatling gun. Derrick's brain spits and burns in synch, working to fix on a way to find them. Cotton probably knows where Rory lives, but he sure as shit won't let it slip to Derrick. He's got a soft spot for the kid, and it doesn't take a psychiatrist to figure out what goes through Derrick's head when he lays eyes on the little asshole. When it comes to violence, Derrick doesn't think much of dilettantes. He's got to know about every kind of violence there is, and there's nothing he wants to do so much as disembowel anybody stupid enough to find meaning in it.

The fights. That's the answer. It's Wednesday, the kid'll be fighting tonight. The Monte Carlo screams into town, kicking slush. Time check. Too late. Derrick cranks the wheel, heads for the bar. Could still catch him.

Then Derrick's head jerks to the side and he hits the brakes. The car slaloms down the blacktop.

He breathes out. He runs his hand down his chin, shifts into reverse, rolls the car backwards. There he is, sitting on the back steps. With a girl. Derrick cracks his window, lights a cigarette. He doesn't bother moving the car so they can't see him. They aren't paying any attention. Their faces buried against each other, the backs of their heads a wall to the world around them. Their reflection spilling onto the blacktop in a monstrous mess of color.

The kid's a pedophile.

When Derrick finally shifts the car into gear and heads down the street, he knows exactly what's coming next.

CHAPTER 72

*~ Go ahead and pick up a cue stick or
something, if you want. ~*

Rory walks. All the way through town, out on 29. Whatever good feeling he caught off Wendy fades quick. He imagines Pike finding out, has to hold his own fist to keep from punching himself in the head. He's disintegrating all over. "Shit," he says under his breath, but the enormity of his stupidity makes the word sound vaporous.

So. He starts to jog. Too drunk, too high. His boots suck snow, his knees crackle, the frigid air burns holes in his lungs. He lifts his legs and picks up his pace. New snow falling around him. A streetlight flickering ribbons of light into the dark. A car slugging through the dirty slush and gone in a gasoline chug and a wash of headlights, frittering down the road.

Then he's out of town, in the parking lot of the Green Frog Café. Then he's inside. Leroy's behind the bar, sipping a Coke, watching John Wayne on the television. "Cotton ain't here."

"I'll take a bourbon."

Leroy eyes him. "I know you?"

"I'm picking up all kinds of bad habits tonight."

"I'll be goddamned." Leroy shakes his head and slides the bourbon to Rory. "And you was my inspiration to quit all mine someday."

The door swings open. Rory ignores it. He swirls his bourbon in his glass, lets it slide down the back of his throat like a snake.

"Cotton ain't here," Leroy says at the door.

"That's good," Derrick answers. "Cotton's gonna have problems with me after tonight."

Rory laughs out loud. He sits his empty shotglass on the bar, points a finger for Leroy to refill it. Derrick takes the stool next to Rory's.

There's a shot of bourbon and a Miller Lite in front of him before he even bothers asking. "I saw you tonight." He lights a cigarette with a match, the flame glimmering a pool of yellow fire on the leathery bar.

"I wasn't worth a shit."

"Not fighting." Derrick drains his shot, hits his cigarette, sets it in the ashtray. "I saw you outside the bar."

Rory glances at him. "And?"

"The first time I met you, you said you fight all takers."

"In the ring. I don't fight outside the ring."

"That's right. Aspiring boxer of the Hemingway variety. Don't want to fuck up all your natural talent brawling in a bar."

"Something like that."

"I been fighting for what's mine since before you were born."

"Come out some Wednesday and see if it's done you any good."

Derrick's left hand sweeps his beer bottle across the bar, smashes it against Rory's head. Rory spins sideways off the stool, blood falling over his eyes like a veil. He cocks his fists, blind, seeing only spots where he can see at all. One of Derrick's fists shoots out of the blackness, clobbers him in the jaw. Rory blinks blood, jerks his head left to right, looking for a target. Another fist. Rips his face sideways, something tearing a gash down his jawline, snagging and cutting free.

Rory stops. Stops breathing, stops moving. He drops his hands without bothering to clear the blood, lets his head clear. He pulls his slamming heart in like a kite, drawing the ragged beats together until they're close and steady.

Derrick's standing in front of him, his hands out to his side and slightly raised. He's grinning a cold snakish grin.

Rory spits a glob of blood on the floor, grins back. "Want to try that again?"

Derrick shuffles his cowboy boots on the hardwood floor and steps with a looping right lead. Rory slips it and blisters a left hook into Derrick's ribs. Derrick drops to one knee.

"Get up," Rory says. He steps back, slapping his hands together. "I cracked a rib, it won't kill you."

Derrick finds his feet and rises slowly, pinning Rory in place with his stare. Then he blinks with pain. Rory's there. Right cross to the temple, jaw clattering uppercut. Rory fades back and Derrick drops to all fours, bleeding from his mouth, choking and coughing on tooth fragments. He stumbles for his feet, makes it to a crouch. Then wobbles and falls back on all fours.

This is fine, Rory thinks, blood pouring down his chin, slicking his sweatshirt and peppering the floor. This is why I fight. It feels good, it feels even, it feels like something I don't ever have to be ashamed of doing. "Go ahead and pick up a cue stick or something, if you want."

Derrick's face darkens and the whole room darkens with it, like the sky's lowered over them. He reaches around his back and pulls his .45.

Rory has a flash of Wendy's face. Just a flash. He can't tell if it's because he's been thinking of her, or because Derrick has a look in his eyes that looks just like hers.

CHAPTER 73

~ *I'll wait here.* ~

*I*t was a late driving salesman who spotted his body bloodying a ditch on 29, just off the logging trail to his shack. The dispatcher was flustered and she ran the report over the air in detail, describing every inch of the body, every wound on him. Then when finished, she began again, as though unable to stop. Then again. This until Jack's voice crackled across the airwaves, "Margaret, shut the fuck up."

Iris doesn't ask any questions when she answers the door to find Wendy standing next to Pike, clutching Monster in her hands, her skinny body twitching with sobs. Just reaches out and pulls the girl gently into her arms, where she crumbles, her face crushed with grief. She's all the sudden a little girl again, ruined and exhausted and in desperate need of someone to take care of her.

"I need you to watch her." Pike stands like a fence post hammered into frozen ground.

"Why?" Iris strokes Wendy's head.

"You sure as hell don't want her to ride with me."

Iris flinches. "Let's get you somewhere where you can lay down," she says gently to Wendy. Then to Pike, in a voice like metal grating on concrete, "You stay right there. Don't you go anywhere." She takes Wendy by the arm and leads her into the house.

"I'll wait here," he lies.

He only makes it one street down from her house when Jack's siren sounds. His breath hisses between his tight lips and he eases the truck to the side of the road. He leans to his glove compartment and pulls out his .357 and sticks it under his leg.

Jack walks cautiously to his window, his right hand drifting to his pistol, unconsciously aware of a danger his brain isn't. He looks thinner. His cheekbones protrude under his heavy eyes and his chin is an axe edge. "You heard it on the scanner, didn't you?" He stands a couple feet back from the truck. "I'm sorry, Pike. He was a hell of a good kid."

"He was."

Jack removes his cowboy hat and runs his fingers through his gray hair and replaces the hat on his head, his eyes everywhere but Pike's. "You know I'll do everything I can to nail the son of a bitch. I'll put every man I can find on it and not one of us will sleep until he's doing time."

"You know better."

An old Chevy slushes down the street past them. Jack looks after it like he wishes he was inside it. Anywhere but where he is. "You know the hell of it? I turned in my resignation yesterday morning. As of two weeks from now, I'm in real estate."

"It's a good move."

"Think you could wait two weeks?"

Pike looks at him.

"I didn't figure." Jack sticks his hands in his pockets and turns his face up at the night. "They'll probably kill you."

"Probably."

"Well. That's your business." Jack exhales a steady stream of frost at the sky. "I'm going home. To bed. If you're still alive when I wake up, don't let me see you in town again. Ever."

"Done."

Pike shifts the truck into gear, drives away.

He used to have to summon up every demon he could muster. His ex, his daughter, every wife-beating junky he ever knew. He was a machine that ran on cocaine and self-hatred. But he doesn't need to work himself up tonight. There are a million reasons to kill Derrick, but none of them matters. Pike's heart is huge and meaty in his chest. He feels it harnessing his blood, mastering it the way you'd master a wild horse. He wheels his truck to a stop in the gravel lot of the Green Frog Café, checking the .357 in his shoulder holster. Then he steps out of the truck and pulls his 30-30 lever-action rifle from behind the seat.

CHAPTER 74

~ It takes two. ~

Leroy's behind the bar, washing a glass, the light under the bar registering a roughneck nobility to his broken nose and jagged jawline. Pike kicks the steel door straight back off its hinges and centers the 30-30's front sight on Leroy's forehead. "Don't."

Leroy does, his hand bolting under the counter. Pike pulls the trigger, blasts his face into a red vapor, the air molecules in the room bursting with the deafening gun blast. Leroy's body folds to the floor, all but headless. Pike levers a new round into the action. Twin retards, Jessie and Jesse, sitting at one of the tables, holding cards. Cotton looking up at him from the pool table at the end of the bar. No Derrick. The twins move fast, tipping up the table, doing their best to hunch behind it. Cotton moves faster, scuttling behind the bar.

Jesse and Jessie first. Pike ducks sideways against the bar, fires a 30-30 round through their table, levers, fires again. The table's thin, Pike hears the rounds smack flesh. A hand pops over the table, raps off three quick shots with a .25 pocket-pistol. None even close. Pike puts another 30-30 round through the table. Jesse falls sideways, Pike puts a bullet in his head.

A thin high screech. Jessie jumps from behind the table, runs at Pike. His hands out-stretched like to strangle him. Pike shoots him the neck, levers, shoots him again center-mass. Doesn't even slow him. Pike drops the empty 30-30, unholsters the .357, fires three rounds into his chest from three feet away. Jessie falls over him, his hands still senselessly groping.

Then a boom. Then a burning in his left arm. Pike catapults over Jessie's body, puts it between himself and the bar. Cotton pumps the 12-gauge, fires again through the bar, the pellets smacking into

Jessie's body. They ain't yet made the shotgun load that can penetrate a three-hundred-pound Kentucky redneck, though. Pike checks his arm. Three or four pellets in the tricep, probably 3 buck. Nothing.

"I count you got three rounds left," Cotton calls from behind the bar, his voice even and languid, muffled by the ringing in Pike's ears.

"I count the same for you," Pike returns. He's laying flat against Jessie's side, Jessie's left arm flapped out above his head, his blood puddling up, lapping against him.

"Might have a whole box of shells back here. You never know."

"Might have a pocketful, myself," Pike says. He blinks, his eyes burning with sweat and cordite.

"Looks like we got a stand-off, outlaw."

"Looks like it."

"I don't believe I ever done anything to you," Cotton says. "I even liked the kid."

"You knew exactly what Derrick was. You put him up."

"Well. He and I have been friends a long time."

"Sure you have." Pike thumbs open the wheel on the .357, reloads it from his pocket. Then scans the floor, doesn't see the 30-30. Must be on the other side of the body.

"You done any thinking on how you're fixing to get out of this?" Cotton says. "Even if you manage to kill me, you're sure to be suspect number one."

"Don't worry about me managing to kill you."

"And don't forget about that little girl. I make a lot of people money. None of them are gonna be happy to see me dead. Revenge killings always seem to spiral that way."

"This ain't a revenge killing," Pike says. "This is a drug deal gone wrong. What do you think the cops'll find when they search this place?"

"Jack'll know better."

"Jack won't give a shit." Pike puts his left toe to the heel of his right cowboy boot, slowly works his foot out.

"Maybe not. But it won't be him alone. You're after Derrick, I'm betting. Cincinnati PD won't take that lying down. They'll come down on this town like a hammer."

"Derrick's crooked. If they investigate too hard they might suck in half the force." Pike's got the right boot off, starts working on the left. "You ain't never gonna lose money counting on crooked cops."

"Fair enough. But you still gotta get past me."

"Sure. But first I'm gonna wait for your buddy to get back. To step into that foyer yonder with the one-way glass. First I'm gonna put him down like a fucking dog. Then I'll hop this bar and put a bullet in you."

"Have it your own way. Got any cigarettes, while we wait?"

Pike fingers a Pall Mall out of his coat pocket and lobs it over the bar. "You get it?"

"I got it."

"Need a light?"

"Got my own."

Pike hears the snick of Cotton's lighter. He slips another cigarette out of his pack and lights it. Then sticks the lit cigarette in Jesse's hand and scoots, as flat as he can, out past Jessie's feet. He swings himself to his feet and pads around the bar.

Cotton's empty boots, a smoking cigarette stuck planted in a shot glass. Cotton down at the other end of the bar, climbing over it barefoot, his back to Pike. Pike cocks the .357. "Looks like we had the same idea," he says.

"Shit," Cotton says. "Well. It was a good one."

"Lay down the shotgun and come on down here."

Cotton does. Sheepishly. "You're gonna ask me where Derrick is, ain't you?"

Pike nods. "Walk over by the pool table."

"Probably wouldn't believe me if I said I didn't know, would you?"

"Probably not," Pike says. "Wanna finish your cigarette?"

"I'm all right."

Pike squeezes the trigger. The room explodes with the boom and Cotton crashes sideways on the floor, his face wild, his hands clutching at the smoking mess that was his left foot. "Stand up," Pike says, his grin as tight as a child-sized coffin.

Cotton huffs air. The bones of his face straining against the skin like it's an elastic mask. He reaches down to his good leg, pulls himself up. He bites a hole all the way through his lip with the effort, a long rivulet of blood dripping from his chin, spattering on the floorboards.

"Walk to the wall and back again."

Cotton does, slathering for air, blowing saliva bubbles, seeming to move by will alone. The shattered bones in his foot scraping the floorboards like fingernails.

"We'll keep on doing laps until you're ready to tell me where Derrick is," Pike says. "If it takes more than three, we'll try it with both your feet blown off."

It takes two.

CHAPTER 75

~ It won't last long. ~

The snow came out of nowhere. Starting light, a flutter of movement crossing the mountains, but now driving through the pass, swirling out in the blackness over the valley. Derrick's spent the last two hours up on Devil's Elbow, sitting in his car with the engine idling, watching the town lights slowly wink out behind the snow-white mask, the darkness. His last night in Nanticonte. He'd meant to say good bye to Cotton, but he didn't. Just told him he needed to sit and think awhile, that he'd back soon. He opens another beer, lights another cigarette.

No sleep. Again. Making up your mind doesn't buy rest. There are no decisions that don't lead to new ones, that don't branch out to others, that don't multiply until they consume your life. Derrick watches the swirling snow. For a long time. Then he stuffs the cigarette butt in his empty beer can, drops it on the floorboard, and opens the car door.

The wind needles his face when he steps out, tearing at his nose. Derrick walks to the edge of the drop-off, stands with his knees against the guard rail. He unzips his pants, pisses an insignificant arc out into the void, zips his pants. He stands for awhile, staring out at the blankness that's taken the place of his home town. Then turns back to his car.

Something punches Derrick in the stomach, a rifle's crack barely audible in the howling wind. It takes Derrick a second or two to make the connection. Then he looks down, sees the hole in his stomach. His knees already sagging, his body a weight beyond his control. He sinks to the ground like a man sinking underwater, reaching for his .45. He can't hold it up. His hand falls on his leg.

Shadows in the snow. Then one shadow detaching from the others, flitting dimly across the expanse. At first indistinct, then taking a human form. Then more than human, stalking towards him, great and shaggy, appearing out of the snow like some kind of elemental the storm's discharging into the world. Then slowly diminishing in size, taking again the shape of a man. Then Pike bends over and takes his .45 out of his hand.

"This is gonna hurt like hell, ain't it?" Derrick says.

Pike hunkers down next to him, holding his father's rifle. "We'll wait for it together."

Derrick nods. Or tries to. There's a pulsing in his ears. Less a sound than a feeling, like the bullet is pounding around his chest cavity in some strangely familiar rhythm. "You know the hell of it?"

"What's that?"

"I was leaving tonight. Heading back to Cincinnati."

Pike runs his hand over the stock of his rifle, looking at it. "It wouldn't have mattered."

The pulse grows, keeps growing. Deafens Derrick so that he can't answer. Then he grins, recognizing it. His heartbeat. He listens to it for a long time. Pike watches over him. Derrick starts counting seconds between the beats. He grins again. "It's pacing down."

Pike lights a cigarette. "What is?"

Derrick holds his shaking hand up for Pike to be silent and listens some more.

Then the pain hits him in a monstrous nauseating wave. Derrick's hand drops, he feels the blood drain out of face, he can't hear his heartbeat at all anymore. "Jesus."

"That it?" Pike asks, blowing smoke.

"I think so," Derrick grunts. "Can we talk about something?"

Pike nods, stubbing the cigarette out in the snow. "Talk to me about my daughter."

So he does. Until he can't anymore.

CHAPTER 76

~ The high hard sun above it all, burning
holes into your brain. ~

Pike drives the backroads all through the night. And then drives through the next day. First through Tennessee, then through Arkansas, until he can barely take anymore. These rolling hills with a slave quarters out back of every farmhouse, where you can't take two steps without grinding an Indian arrowhead under your boot. And not a small town to drive through that he can bring himself to stop in.

But then the land starts to clear. And then it is clear. And finally he's on the West Texas plains. The road opening through the tallgrass like a black flag unfurling in the wind, the sunlight spilling over the truck like a warm wash of water. He lights a cigarette and cracks the window. The desert air circles through the cab of the truck, dry and clean. It breaks over Pike's face like a stream breaking over a stone outcropping.

He's been driving for twenty-three hours straight. But when he ashes in the Styrofoam cup between his legs, his movements are easy and his eyes are alert and relaxed. The lack of sleep has loosened his joints, lightened the weight of his muscles. He lets the smoke float out of him like some wild bird he's released from his cupped hands. He doesn't think he's ever been more tired. And he doesn't think he's ever been less likely to sleep.

West Texas can seem like it runs on forever. It's a landscape Pike knows and loves. Lean and bleak, populated with blasted trees, it's hard to imagine anywhere else on earth as desolate. For the melancholy feeling, maybe an abandoned cemetery, especially if you've known someone buried there. Or a city crumbling into ruin, decimated by centuries of neglect and the kind of hatred that rots you from the inside out. For the solitude, maybe the crags and forests of the Great Divide, or the blue frozen wastes of the Poles. But you won't find anything like West Texas for the combination of the two. It never changes, it never will. Any crop planted begins to wither off from the moment the soil's turned, and there's a lonesomeness that stalks through the tallgrass like a predator. It's a landscape meant to remind you that everyone has a hollow feeling they can't handle. That the only trick to living your life is not to destroy yourself trying to shake it.

The sky lowers as he drives, and he watches a black cloudbank form, miles ahead. The air crackles and sparks and lightning splinters a lone tree standing up out of the bowed grass. Then the looming horizon cracks violently in two and rain breaks out, washing over the plains in a great deluge. They drive into it.

Pike finishes his cigarette and drops the butt into his coffee. Then his hand moves across the seat, past Wendy's tossed black hair, to pull his work coat up on her shoulder. Monster lays with his proud little face rested against her chin. They drive through the rain, then come out on the other side of it, back into the burning sun.

She wakes long enough to stop for a bathroom break alongside the highway. Pike lifts a garbage sack with the clothes he'd been wearing and a five-gallon can of gasoline out of the truck and walks back on the plains while she pisses in the dirt. He kicks through the dust and the sand sage, the high hard sun burning down into the back of his neck. When he finds a clear patch of ground, he scuffs out a shallow indentation with his boot, tosses the garbage bag in, and empties the can of gasoline over it. Then he lights a dead mesquite twig with his Zippo and tosses it on the heap. Flame whooshes up and a cloud of black oily smoke plumes skyward.

Pike walks back a little further into the desert while it burns. In a mesquite tree clearing he finds a mother pig and a drift of sucklings. He hunkers down on his heels and watches them suckle. Then, when the smoke has died down and the fire played out, he returns to his pit, makes sure everything has burnt, and scatters the ashes. Then he turns back to his truck, where Wendy is already asleep again.

And the West Texas plains keep rolling out in front of him. And they keep unwinding out into the horizon, like the consequences

PIKE

of his younger self, like the concussions of his own past that keep reverberating back to him. He's let them rip at his mind until he can't tell the monsters he's invented from the monsters that walked in and out of his youth, and it's only on these plains that he realizes it doesn't matter. Time slips away, and he lets it.

What lives here lives in the sun. There's nothing you can hide under and no way to escape it. There's no shade and no cover on these plains, and when storms hit you don't hide, you just stand still and hope the lightning doesn't blast you out of your skin. And though the plains seem like they'll never end, they do. They cross a wide, cool river, and they roll right on into Mexico.

EPILOGUE

A kitchen. An exhausted blonde woman sitting at a Formica kitchen table that's marred all over with cigarette burns. She's wearing a pair of jeans and a white Myrtle Beach T-shirt, smoking a cigarette. In the bedroom, the twins are down for the night. For now. She's got her bed made up on the couch and the dishes done. The cigarette is her last for the night.

And tomorrow she has to take the bus to Kroger's with the twins and make it back with enough groceries to last the week. Enough for her brothers, too, who stop in for breakfast every morning and expect it ready. And the bathroom needs cleaning. The twins play in there and her brothers have pissed a halo around the toilet.

The exhaustion feels like a bone cancer eating at her skeleton. Like the day-to-day thinness of her life has rotted out her marrow. When she moves, her joints grind against each other.

Outside, above the crumbling redbricks and smokestacks of Cincinnati, a sliver of the moon is there. Thin, silvery, wavering in the night air. There are stars, too, but they're invisible in the glare and the smog that lies cracked over the city like a jigsaw puzzle of varying shades of gray. She stares out into the night, smoking, her eyes wavering with pain. For a minute she thinks of her Bogie and she misses him terribly. To have someone on her side.

Holding the cigarette in her thin claw like hand, she punches it out on her forearm just for thinking it. Her skin sizzles and burns.

Outside nothing changes. Inside too.

THE END

ABOUT THE AUTHOR

Benjamin Whitmer was born in 1972 and raised on back-to-the-land communes and counterculture enclaves ranging from Southern Ohio to Upstate New York. One of his earliest and happiest memories is of standing by the side of a country road with his mother, hitchhiking to parts unknown. Since then, he has been a factory grunt, a vacuum salesman, a convalescent, a high-school dropout, a semi-truck loader, an activist, a kitchen-table gunsmith, a squatter, a college professor, a dishwasher, a technical writer, and a petty thief. He has also published fiction and non-fiction in a number of magazines, anthologies, and essay collections. *Pike* is his first novel.

PM PRESS was founded at the end of 2007 by a small collection of folks with decades of publishing, media, and organizing experience. PM co-founder Ramsey Kanaan started AK Press as a young teenager in Scotland almost 30 years ago and, together with his fellow PM Press co-conspirators, has published and distributed hundreds of books, pamphlets, CDs, and DVDs. Members of PM have founded enduring book fairs, spearheaded victorious tenant organizing campaigns, and worked closely with bookstores, academic conferences, and even rock bands to deliver political and challenging ideas to all walks of life. We're old enough to know what we're doing and young enough to know what's at stake.

We seek to create radical and stimulating fiction and non-fiction books, pamphlets, t-shirts, visual and audio materials to entertain, educate and inspire you. We aim to distribute these through every available channel with every available technology - whether that means you are seeing anarchist classics at our bookfair stalls; reading our latest vegan cookbook at the café; downloading geeky fiction e-books; or digging new music and timely videos from our website.

PM Press is always on the lookout for talented and skilled volunteers, artists, activists and writers to work with. If you have a great idea for a project or can contribute in some way, please get in touch.

PM PRESS • PO BOX 23912 • OAKLAND, CA 94623
www.pmpress.org

FRIENDS OF PM PRESS

These are indisputably momentous times — the financial system is melting down globally and the Empire is stumbling. Now more than ever there is a vital need for radical ideas.

In the year since its founding — and on a mere shoestring — PM Press has risen to the formidable challenge of publishing and distributing knowledge and entertainment for the struggles ahead. With over 75 releases to date, we have published an impressive and stimulating array of literature, art, music, politics, and culture. Using every available medium, we've succeeded in connecting those hungry for ideas and information to those putting them into practice.

Friends of PM allows you to directly help impact, amplify, and revitalize the discourse and actions of radical writers, filmmakers, and artists. It provides us with a stable foundation from which we can build upon our early successes and provides a much-needed subsidy for the materials that can't necessarily pay their own way. You can help make that happen — and receive every new title automatically delivered to your door once a month — by joining as a Friend of PM Press. And, we'll throw in a free T-Shirt when you sign up.

Here are your options:

- **$25 a month** Get all books and pamphlets plus 50% discount on all webstore purchases

- **$25 a month** Get all CDs and DVDs plus 50% discount on all webstore purchases

- **$40 a month** Get all PM Press releases plus 50% discount on all webstore purchases

- **$100 a month Superstar** — Everything plus PM merchandise, free downloads, and 50% discount on all webstore purchases

For those who can't afford $25 or more a month, we're introducing Sustainer Rates at $15, $10 and $5. Sustainers get a free PM Press t-shirt and a 50% discount on all purchases from our website.

Your Visa or Mastercard will be billed once a month, until you tell us to stop. Or until our efforts succeed in bringing the revolution around. Or the financial meltdown of Capital makes plastic redundant. Whichever comes first.

More from SWITCHBLADE

The Jook
Gary Phillips

ISBN: 978-1-60486-040-5
256 pages $15.95

Zelmont Raines has slid a long way since his ability to jook,
to out maneuver his opponents on the field, made him a
Super Bowl winning wide receiver, earning him lucrative
endorsement deals and more than his share of female
attention. But Zee hasn't always been good at saying no, so
a series of missteps involving drugs, a paternity suit or two,
legal entanglements, shaky investments and recurring injuries have virtually sidelined
his career.

That is until Los Angeles gets a new pro franchise, the Barons, and Zelmont has
one last chance at the big time he dearly misses. Just as it seems he might be getting
back in the flow, he's enraptured by Wilma Wells, the leggy and brainy lawyer for the
team—who has a ruthless game plan all her own. And it's Zelmont who might get
jooked.

"Phillips, author of the acclaimed Ivan Monk series, takes elements of Jim
Thompson (the ending), black-exploitation flicks (the profanity-fueled dialogue),
and *Penthouse* magazine (the sex is anatomically correct) to create an over-the-top
violent caper in which there is no honor, no respect, no love, and plenty of money.
Anyone who liked George Pelecanos' *King Suckerman* is going to love this even-
grittier take on many of the same themes." — Wes Lukowsky, *Booklist*

"Enough gritty gossip, blistering action and trash talk to make real life L.A. seem
comparatively wholesome." — Kirkus Reviews

"Gary Phillips writes tough and gritty parables about life and death on the mean
streets—a place where sometimes just surviving is a noble enough cause. His is a
voice that should be heard and celebrated. It rings true once again in *The Jook*, a
story where all of Phillips' talents are on display." — Michael Connelly, author of the
Harry Bosch books

I-5
Summer Brenner

ISBN: 978-1-60486-019-1
256 pages $15.95

A novel of crime, transport, and sex, *I-5* tells the bleak
and brutal story of Anya and her journey north from Los
Angeles to Oakland on the interstate that bisects the Central
Valley of California.

Anya is the victim of a deep deception. Someone has
lied to her; and because of this lie, she is kept under lock and
key, used by her employer to service men, and indebted for the privilege. In exchange,
she lives in the United States and fantasizes on a future American freedom. Or as she
remarks to a friend, "Would she rather be fucking a dog… or living like a dog?" In
Anya's world, it's a reasonable question.

Much of *I-5* transpires on the eponymous interstate. Anya travels with her
"manager" and driver from Los Angeles to Oakland. It's a macabre journey: a drop at
Denny's, a bad patch of fog, a visit to a "correctional facility," a rendezvous with an
organ grinder, and a dramatic entry across Oakland's city limits.

"Insightful, innovative and riveting. After its lyrical beginning inside Anya's head,
I-5 shifts momentum into a rollicking gangsters-on-the-lam tale that is in turns
blackly humorous, suspenseful, heartbreaking and always populated by intriguing
characters. Anya is a wonderful, believable heroine, her tragic tale told from the
inside out, without a shred of sentimental pity, which makes it all the stronger. A
twisty, fast-paced ride you won't soon forget." — Denise Hamilton, author of the
L.A.*Times* bestseller *The Last Embrace*.

"I'm in awe. *I-5* moves so fast you can barely catch your breath. It's as tough as tires,
as real and nasty as road rage, and best of all, it careens at breakneck speed over as
many twists and turns as you'll find on The Grapevine. What a ride! *I-5*'s a hardboiled standout." — Julie Smith, editor of *New Orleans Noir* and author of the Skip
Langdon and Talba Wallis crime novel series

"In *I-5*, Summer Brenner deals with the onerous and gruesome subject of sex
trafficking calmly and forcefully, making the reader feel the pain of its victims. The
trick to forging a successful narrative is always in the details, and *I-5* provides them
in abundance. This book bleeds truth — after you finish it, the blood will be on your
hands." — Barry Gifford, author, poet and screenwriter

The Chieu Hoi Saloon
Michael Harris

ISBN: 978-1-60486-112-9
320 pages $19.95

It's 1992 and three people's lives are about to collide against the flaming backdrop of the Rodney King riots in Los Angeles. Vietnam vet Harry Hudson is a journalist fleeing his past: the war, a failed marriage, and a fear-ridden childhood. Rootless, he stutters, wrestles with depression, and is aware he's passed the point at which victim becomes victimizer. He explores the city's lowest dives, the only places where he feels at home. He meets Mama Thuy, a Vietnamese woman struggling to run a Navy bar in a tough Long Beach neighborhood, and Kelly Crenshaw, an African-American prostitute whose husband is in prison. They give Harry insight that maybe he can do something to change his fate in a gripping story that is both a character study and thriller.

"Mike Harris' novel has all the brave force and arresting power of Celine and Dostoevsky in its descent into the depths of human anguish and that peculiar gallantry of the moral soul that is caught up in irrational self-punishment at its own failings. Yet Harris manages an amazing and transforming affirmation — the novel floats above all its pain on pure delight in the variety of the human condition. It is a story of those sainted souls who live in bars, retreating from defeat but rendered with such vividness and sensitivity that it is impossible not to care deeply about these figures from our own waking dreams. In an age less obsessed by sentimentality and mawkish 'uplift,' this book would be studied and celebrated and emulated." — John Shannon, author of *The Taking of the Waters* and the Jack Liffey mysteries

"Michael Harris is a realist with a realist's unflinching eye for the hard truths of contemporary times. Yet in *The Chieu Hoi Saloon*, he gives us a hero worth admiring: the passive, overweight, depressed and sex-obsessed Harry Hudson, who in the face of almost overwhelming despair still manages to lead a valorous life of deep faith. In this powerful and compelling first novel, Harris makes roses bloom in the gray underworld of porno shops, bars and brothels by compassionately revealing the yearning loneliness beneath the grime — our universal human loneliness that seeks transcendence through love." — Paula Huston, author of *Daughters of Song* and *The Holy Way*

"*The Chieu Hoi Saloon* concerns one Harry Hudson, the literary bastard son of David Goodis and Dorothy Hughes. Hardcore and unsparing, the story takes you on a ride with Harry in his bucket of a car and pulls you into his subterranean existence in bright daylight and gloomy shadow. One sweet read." — Gary Phillips, author of *The Jook*

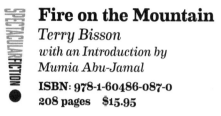

Fire on the Mountain
Terry Bisson
with an Introduction by
Mumia Abu-Jamal
ISBN: 978-1-60486-087-0
208 pages $15.95

It's 1959 in socialist Virginia. The Deep South is an independent Black nation called Nova Africa. The second Mars expedition is about to touch down on the red planet. And a pregnant scientist is climbing the Blue Ridge in search of her great-great grandfather, a teenage slave who fought with John Brown and Harriet Tubman's guerrilla army.

Long unavailable in the US, published in France as *Nova Africa*, *Fire on the Mountain* is the story of what might have happened if John Brown's raid on Harper's Ferry had succeeded—and the Civil War had been started not by the slave owners but the abolitionists.

"History revisioned, turned inside out ... Bisson's wild and wonderful imagination has taken some strange turns to arrive at such a destination." — Madison Smartt Bell, Anisfield-Wolf Award winner and author of *Devil's Dream*

"You don't forget Bisson's characters, even well after you've finished his books. His *Fire on the Mountain* does for the Civil War what Philip K. Dick's *The Man in the High Castle* did for World War Two." — George Alec Effinger, winner of the Hugo and Nebula awards for *Shrödinger's Kitten*, and author of the Marîd Audran trilogy.

"A talent for evoking the joyful, vertiginous experiences of a world at fundamental turning points." — *Publishers Weekly*

"Few works have moved me as deeply, as thoroughly, as Terry Bisson's *Fire On The Mountain*... With this single poignant story, Bisson molds a world as sweet as banana cream pies, and as briny as hot tears." — Mumia Abu-Jamal, death row prisoner and author of *Live From Death Row*, from the Introduction.

FOUND IN
TRANSLATION **from PM Press**

Calling All Heroes:
A Manual for Taking Power
Paco Ignacio Taibo II
ISBN: 978-1-60486-205-8
128 pages $12.00

The euphoric idealism of grassroots reform and the tragic
reality of revolutionary failure are at the center of this
speculative novel that opens with a real historical event. On
October 2, 1968, 10 days before the Summer Olympics in
Mexico, the Mexican government responds to a student
demonstration in Tlatelolco by firing into the crowd, killing more than 200 students
and civilians and wounding hundreds more. The massacre of Tlatelolco was erased
from the official record as easily as authorities washing the blood from the streets, and
no one was ever held accountable.

It is two years later and Nestor, a journalist and participant in the fateful events,
lies recovering in the hospital from a knife wound. His fevered imagination leads
him in the collection of facts and memories of the movement and its assassination
in the company of figures from his childhood. Nestor calls on the heroes of his
youth — Sherlock Holmes, Doc Holliday, Wyatt Earp and D'Artagnan among them — to
join him in launching a new reform movement conceived by his intensely active
imagination.

"Taibo's writing is witty, provocative, finely nuanced and well worth the
challenge." — Publishers Weekly

"I am his number one fan... I can always lose myself in one of his novels because of
their intelligence and humor. My secret wish is to become one of the characters in
his fiction, all of them drawn from the wit and wisdom of popular imagination. Yet
make no mistake, Paco Taibo—sociologist and historian—is recovering the political
history of Mexico to offer a vital, compelling vision of our reality." — Laura Esquivel,
author of *Like Water for Chocolate*

"The real enchantment of Mr. Taibo's storytelling lies in the wild and melancholy
tangle of life he sees everywhere." — *New York Times Book Review*

"It doesn't matter what happens. Taibo's novels constitute an absurdist manifesto.
No matter how oppressive a government, no matter how strict the limitations
of life, we all have our imaginations, our inventiveness, our ability to liven up
lonely apartments with a couple of quacking ducks. If you don't have anything left,
oppressors can't take anything away." — *Washington Post Book World*

Lonely Hearts Killer
Tomoyuki Hoshino

ISBN: 978-1-60486-084-9
288 pages $15.95

What happens when a popular and young emperor suddenly dies, and the only person available to succeed him is his sister? How can people in an island country survive as climate change and martial law are eroding more and more opportunities for local sustainability and mutual aid? And what can be done to challenge the rise of a new authoritarian political leadership at a time when the general public is obsessed with fears related to personal and national "security"? These and other provocative questions provide the backdrop for this powerhouse novel about young adults embroiled in what appear to be more private matters – friendships, sex, a love suicide, and struggles to cope with grief and work.

PM Press is proud to bring you this first English translation of a full-length novel by the award-winning author Tomoyuki Hoshino.

"A major novel by Tomoyuki Hoshino, one of the most compelling and challenging writers in Japan today, *Lonely Hearts Killer* deftly weaves a path between geopolitical events and individual experience, forcing a personal confrontation with the political brutality of the postmodern era. Adrienne Hurley's brilliant translation captures the nuance and wit of Hoshino's exploration of depths that rise to the surface in the violent acts of contemporary youth." — Thomas LaMarre, William Dawson Professor of East Asian Studies, McGill University

"Since his debut, Hoshino has used as the core of his writing a unique sense of the unreality of things, allowing him to illuminate otherwise hidden realities within Japanese society. And as he continues to write from this tricky position, it goes without saying that he produces work upon work of extraordinary beauty and power." — Yuko Tsushima, award-winning Japanese novelist

"Reading Hoshino's novels is like traveling to a strange land all by yourself. You touch down on an airfield in a foreign country, get your passport stamped, and leave the airport all nerves and anticipation. The area around an airport is more or less the same in any country. It is sterile and without character. There, you have no real sense of having come somewhere new. But then you take a deep breath and a smell you've never encountered enters your nose, a wind you've never felt brushes against your skin, and an unknown substance rains down upon your head." — Mitsuyo Kakuta, award-winning Japanese novelist

Geek Mafia:
Black Hat Blues
Rick Dakan

ISBN: 978-1-60486-088-7
272 pages $17.95

What do you call 1000 hackers assembled into one hotel
for the weekend? A menace to society? Trouble waiting to
happen? They call it a computer security conference, or
really, a Hacker Con. A place for hackers, security experts,
penetration testers, and tech geeks of all stripes to gather
and discuss the latest hack, exploits, and gossip. For Paul,
Chloe, and their Crew of con artist vigilantes, it's the perfect hunting ground for their
most ambitious plans yet.

After a year of undercover recruiting at hacker cons all over the country, Chloe
and Paul have assembled a new Crew of elite hackers, driven anarchist activists, and
seductive impersonators. Under the cover of one of the Washington DC's biggest and
most prestigious hacker events, they're going up against power house lobbyists, black
hat hackers, and even the U.S. Congress in order to take down their most challenging,
and most deserving target yet. The stakes have never been higher for them, and
who knows if their new recruits are up to the immense challenge of undermining
"homeland security" for the greater good.

Inspired by years of author Rick Dakan's research in the hacker community, *Geek
Mafia: Black Hat Blues* opens a new, self-contained chapter in the techno-thriller series.

**"Filled with charming geek humor, thoroughly likable characters, and a relentless
plot..."** — Cory Doctorow, co-editor of *BoingBoing*, on the Geek Mafia books"

**"A first rate example of geek fiction getting it right. *Black Hat Blues* gives new
meaning to the term 'hacker con'—you won't want to put it down."** — Heidi Potter,
Shmoocon organizer

**"Rick Dakan is one of the few fiction authors working today who tries to understand
hacker culture not as a sideshow or scare tactic, but as a way of living a life. His
words ring with honest research."** — Jason Scott, director of *BBS: The Documentary*